Roger Pulvers is an author, playwright, theater director, translator and filmmaker. He has published more than fifty books in Japanese and English, including novels, essays, plays, and poetry. Working as assistant to director Nagisa Oshima on *Merry Christmas, Mr. Lawrence* brought him back to Japan and inspired him to become the award-winning playwright, film director and prolific author he is today. His novel, *Hoshizuna Monogatari (Star Sand)*, which he wrote in Japanese, was published by Kodansha, Japan's largest publisher, in 2015, and subsequently in English and French in 2016 and 2017 respectively. It was released as a film, directed by him, in 2017. His most recent books are the novels, *Half of Each Other* and *Peaceful Circumstances*, and his autobiography, *The Unmaking of an American*, all published by Balestier Press.

ALSO BY ROGER PULVERS

The Dream of Lafcadio Hearn
Liv
The Unmaking of an American
Peaceful Circumstances
Half of Each Other

ROGER PULVERS

THE HONEY AND THE FIRES

ancient stories retold for our time

BALESTIER PRESS
LONDON · SINGAPORE

Balestier Press
Centurion House, London TW18 4AX
www.balestier.com

The Honey and the Fires

Stories 1-12 first published by ABC Books, Australia in 2006
This edition first published by Balestier Press in 2019

A CIP catalogue record for this book
is available from the British Library.

ISBN 978 1 911221 36 4

Cover illustration by Alice Pulvers

To Susan

who has taught me more than she will ever imagine

And for our children

Jeremy, Alice, Sophie and Lucy

And for our grandchildren

Hannah, Christopher, Nicholas, Thomas, James and Holly

Why do the nations conspire

and the peoples plot in vain?

The Book of Psalms 2:1

The Stories

THE HANDWRITING ON THE WALL

1. In the Mind of the King

I have been unduly and greatly troubled by my dreams.
During the day I impose a perfect order on all circumstances.
My people act according to my wishes.
Events unfold like silk on marble, smoothly and propitiously.
I am a great king.
I must be so, because all people under my power say so.

Life under me has not always been peaceful.
There were people who dared to disobey by questioning me.
I did not kill all of them, as my priests would have had me do.
For the scholars who defied me with glib erudition, there was exile.
There I left them to harass the dumb ears of aliens to their heart's
      bitter content.
For the laborers who provoked me with a refusal to work, there was
      the dungeon.
There I abandoned them to test their contempt against the putrid
      stone of walls.
(After all, I happily told myself, is this not what walls are for?)

For the women who withheld themselves from me, there was the
      army.
I donated the women to protest in the teeth of a hundred half-
      stripped warriors.

As the years passed and my wisdom grew, swollen by the sayings
        of my ever-loyal priests,
defiance disappeared,
provocation died out,
and protestations against my will ceased to be so much as a
        memory.
The silence of my subjects was music to my ears.

But at night, in my wise and magnanimous old age,
the humans and fiends inhabiting my mind began to spurn me.
I could not control them.
Even waking from sleep did not kill them off.
I called in my servants, who ran about the room strangulating the
        air.
I summoned my priests, who choked it with perfumed smoke.
I commanded my executioners to chop at it with sharpened
        hatchets.
But the humans and fiends born of my mind survived,
flitting through the air from constricting fists, fragrant incense
        and flashing blades.
Was there no one who would rid me of these unruly elements?

Night after night men and women peeled the skin from my flesh,
dogs and cats went mad, salivating over my eyeballs,
and beasts of a grotesque description stood on their hind legs
        inside my mouth,
spitting the poison of laughter down my throat.
I awoke flailing my arms, scratching my eyes and expelling a sick
        bile from between my teeth.
I had priests suffocate the servants and executioners decapitate
        the priests.
I even rotated executioners, kicking the old ones off high cliffs.

I had my hundred wives tied up in muslin bags with starving
    snakes and discarded them into deep wells.
And yet, despite all my best efforts,
from night to night and encroaching day
my nightmares returned
with a vengeance all their own.
My sages, with their unhelpful saws,
my advisors, always agreeably facile,
and my priests, dripping with sanguine prophecies,
failed me down to the last fool.
I would have gladly brought my scholars back from exile were
    they not all feebleminded or dead.
I would have gleefully opened the schools that I closed were there
    any teachers alive to teach in them.
I would even eagerly adopt a new religion for myself and my
    subjects
if such a thing would grant me peace in this life
and guarantee eternal bliss in the next.
But damned nightmares were depriving me of moderate reason,
preventing me from making desirable improvements to social
    policy!
A king can treat a people in any manner he desires
so long as there is order in his mind.

Then I was told of a youth named Daniel, whose people had been
    subjugated.
Daniel had been captured as a young man and groomed into
    obeisance.
I was informed of his gift of interpretation,
an ability to decipher the arbitrary code of dreams.
I will call in this youth and command him to make sense of my
    darkly disordered mind.

Once order reigns in my mind, harmony will return to my land.
The two are one and the same.

2. The Dream of the Statue

Daniel stood before the king, who offered the young man a
      tableful of sweet foods.
He provided him the ten youngest of his women, to pass the time
      with them as he saw fit.
He waved a priest's garb in front of Daniel's face, saying …
"After you have partaken of the sweetness of these foods and the
      flesh of these women,
this white robe is yours to wear till your dying day
and yours for a coffin's pall forever after.
No man in his right mind would refuse such a proposition."
Daniel waved his hand in front of his face, which the king rightly
      interpreted as a dismissal of wants.
"How much gold and silver will you accept
to make sense of the wicked thoughts in my mind?"
Daniel shook his head, which the king correctly interpreted as a
      rejection of wealth.
The king was at wits' end.
Never had he met such a man as Daniel.
He slumped into his throne and scratched his scalp.
This caused his crown, studded with diamonds and other stolen
      precious stones,
to topple onto his shoulder and bounce over his arm.
Daniel jumped forward, catching the crown in his open fingers.
He stood before the king, holding the dazzling crown high into
      the air and said …
"Last night you saw the dream of a statue."

The king jerked his head from one side to the other, biting his lower lip with his upper teeth, breathing in short heavy breaths, and searching the expressions of his priests and advisors for help.

Then he spoke …

"Yes … I did. I did!"

Daniel continued …

"This statue has the face of a devil.

It towers over all the other statues and manmade structures of your kingdom.

Its head of pure gold is so radiant that those who gaze up at it in the heat of day are blinded by its reflection.

Its torso and arms of gleaming silver are so imposing that those who do not prostrate themselves before it are struck with indelible dread.

Its waist and pelvis of bronze are so hard that no missile, of whatever composition, can so much as dent its surface.

Its legs of iron are a sign of the strength of your majesty's power.

But its feet … its feet …"

"Yes, what about its feet?! Tell me about its feet!" cried the king, now standing and shaking his fingers in the air.

Daniel continued …

"Well, its feet are made of clay. And this means …"

"What does it mean?! You must tell me!" pleaded the king, his knees knocking together under his bright yellow ermine gown.

"I'm just getting to that," said Daniel, handing the king his crown.

"No, I don't want that now. Just tell me what the meaning of the feet is, for heaven's sake!

I am leader of the greatest empire that history has ever known.

I want to know the one thing that I cannot discover by myself."

This was the first time in the king's long reign that he admitted to
        needing the mercy of another person.
Daniel hesitated.
"You may not like the answer that I give you."
"No matter. So long as it is the true answer."
This, too, was the first time in the king's long reign he admitted
        that truth might differ from an imposed reality.
"Well, as for the feet … well, uh, you see …"
"Get to it, I tell you!" shouted the king, frantically shifting his
        slight weight from one foot to the other.
"Get to the damn feet!"
And having said that, the king fell to the floor, sat in front of
        Daniel and crossed his legs.

Daniel knelt, put the crown in the king's lap and continued …
"Well, you see, the feet of clay mean simply that the days of your
        kingdom's reign are numbered."
"NO!" cried the king.
"Oh yes," said Daniel. "You see, the clay is there as a warning
that no ruler can rule forever without the consent of the ruled.
Their silence will eventually undermine you.
They will bring you to your knees.
Their acquiescence is your feet of clay."
"NO! NO! NO!" shrieked the king with his head in the vice of his
        hands.
The king then stared around the room.
The room was lined with his priests and advisors, plastered against
        the wall like ancient chairs.
They too were silent, for they did not know whether to contradict
        Daniel or applaud him,
not until they had the final word from the king on the subject.
The king stood up,

and, without saying another word,
laid his crown carefully on the seat of his throne.

Then, with his hands at his sides and his head bowed,
he made his strutting exit,
a tragic actor on a stage of his own design.

3. The Handwriting on the Wall

But that wasn't the end of the matter by any means.
That night, the king had no bad dreams.
In fact, he didn't dream of anything at all.
Ah, the luxury of a dreamless sleep!
When he awoke he was shocked and pleasantly surprised.
He called in his priests and advisors to tell them the happy news
        that his mind was no longer in disarray.
The priests and advisors were profoundly relieved to hear this.
A further disarray in the king's mind could trigger the cruel and
        sudden death of any number of them.
So the king ordered a public holiday throughout his land,
banning the discussion of dreams.
He naturally had Daniel arrested and thrown into the lion's den,
placing a massive stone over it to prevent escape.
He feasted like a king, for after all, that was the privilege of kings
        in those days,
indulged in as much nighttime pleasure as his age permitted,
and promptly fell asleep with a blissful smile on his lips.

But no sooner had the black of sleep overcome him than did a
        wicked vision appear on its taut curtain.
He bolted up, screaming.

"It's come back!
Open the lion's den!
Summon Daniel!
I must have Daniel here this instant!"
He moaned and groaned, whined and sniffled, wriggled and kicked.
He tore small ovals of hair from his scalp and flung them against the
    walls of his bed chamber.

As luck would have it Daniel had not yet been eaten by the lions.
Apparently they had no appetite for him.
They just lolled about in the corner of the den, burping and
    belching.
(It is said that Daniel's friends had prepared poisoned meat for him
    to take into the den, but this has never been confirmed.)
"What's the problem now?" asked Daniel, entering the king's bed
    chamber.
"A dream! A dream! I had another dream!"
"But, sire," said the king's head priest, "you must not discuss dreams.
It's against the law."
"Shut up, you idiot!" yelled the king. "Laws don't apply to me!"
Daniel approached the king's trembling bed and took his hand in
    his.
"Very nice rings you have, your majesty," said Daniel.
"Oh, thank you. You see these stones? They are from your … what?
Forget the rings! Just tell me what I saw in my dream!"
The king was now begging Daniel to relieve him of the curse of his
    dream.

"Well," said Daniel, dropping the king's hand and pacing around the
    bed in a deliberate manner,

"I am afraid this dream is the worst one of all. Are you sure that you really want to know its meaning?"

"Yes … yes … YES! I am going mad from these dreams. Only you can stop me from having them."

"Okay. But I warn you, you won't like what I am going to say."

The king cringed, sitting with his back flush against the bedhead, and tightly embraced his huge goose-down pillow.

Daniel interpreted the king's dream for him in this way …

"There is a wall in your dream.

Isn't there?"

The king, bleary eyed and in a daze, nodded, and continued to nod as Daniel revealed the dream to him.

"There are four words written on your wall.

Nobody here knows how they got there.

Nobody here knows what they mean.

Perhaps some person wrote them in the dead of night …

a young man who is yet unknown

a captured woman far from home

an old man who never gave in,

his conscience his sole haven.

You see, not even the king of the greatest nation that the world has ever known can read words that appear from nowhere."

"But what do they mean?"

"The four words? They mean …

number number weight divisions."

"Number number weight divisions?" said the king, arching his eyebrows.

"Number number weight divisions?" repeated his priests and advisors in unison.

"Yes," said Daniel.

"Then I must be going crazy," chuckled the king, amused at the
absurdity of his dream.

The priests and advisors chuckled too, if half under their breath.

"It is more ominous a dream than your laughter would suggest, your
majesty," continued Daniel.

"It means that the days of your empire will soon be a thing of the
past."

"The past?"

"Yes, the past."

"But why does the word 'number' appear twice on the wall?" asked
the king.

And Daniel replied …

"Emphasis.

Sometimes people who write these things are trying to make a
point."

"But what of 'weight'?" asked the king, his entire body shuddering.

"You have been weighed on the scales of justice, your majesty, and
have been found too light."

"Too light?"

"Yes."

"And the last word … in the handwriting on the wall?" asked the
king in a whisper of breath.

"Your empire will be divided, for it has become too powerful for its
own good."

Having said that, Daniel left.

The king stared around the room with eyes of clouded glass,
unable to move … and unable to speak.

His priests and advisors were pinned to the walls like terrified
statues.

The king went down in history,
not only as it is interpreted in the Bible,
as a supremely evil man
whose kingdom did not survive long past his death.

But one thing in this story has remained unclear to this day.
It is not known whether the ruler of the most powerful nation in the
        history of the world actually dreamt those dreams or not,
or whether Daniel, with his gifts of description, had envisioned
        them for him …
or if Daniel, too, was not a fiction of a mind's imagination.

The germ of the demise of a nation has its origin in its rulers' mind,
        cultured in their own hand, spread by their lust for power.
It is the mind, too, that harbors the cure.

If anything is true about the story of the handwriting on the wall …
        it is this.

NOAH'S ARK

1. The Gathering Storm

The sun was still shining when it all began.
Birds sailed through the air without a care in the world.
Turtles toddled over the ground.
Whales and the fishes of the sea plunged and swam, plunged and
  swam.
And all the animals stood proud and tall,
happy to be living on this Earth.
Only the humans were never satisfied with the home nature had
  given them.
They fought with each other like cats and dogs.
They ruined the beautiful forests, cutting down trees like eager
  beavers.
They stuffed themselves, eating like horses,
while others starved.
They destroyed nature like …
well, like only human beings can.
But there was a good man, and his name was Noah.
Noah saw how his fellow humans were ruining the air, water and
  land,
and he said to his wife, Mrs. Noah …
"Oh, things are not good on this Earth.
A great disaster is awaiting us.
I feel it in my bones."

And having said that, Noah looked up to the sky and shivered.
He saw the storm coming before anyone else.
He knew that this would be a storm like no other,
one that would swallow up life itself.
So Noah asked his wife and their three sons and their three wives to
        help build an ark.
"Let us build the ark so that all creatures will have a future on
        Earth."

Now, Noah's ark was not just your ordinary ark.
First of all, it was absolutely enormous, a world in itself.
It had to be enormous to fit in all the creatures to be saved.
Second of all, it had lots of decks and rooms and pools.
But most important of all, being an ark, it had an enormous roof.
Without a roof the ark would be flooded
and nobody would have been left to write this story.

So Noah, his wife, his three sons and their three wives
set about to build the ark.

They measured and they sawed.
They measured again and they hammered.
And all the while Noah looked up into the sky,
and with his bones shivering inside his body, he said …
"Our time is running out.
There is a great storm gathering on the horizon!"
Noah, his wife, their three sons and their three wives
now began to work as if their lives depended on it.
They measured and they sawed for dear life.
They measured again and they hammered again

with only the ark in their mind.
Other humans there were not impressed.
"The Noahs are fools to work so hard for nothing!" they cried.
And, shrugging their shoulders, they turned their back on them and
	left.
Noah cried out, with his eyes on heaven …
"Hurry, hurry! We have no time to lose."
They worked harder and harder, faster and faster, to build the ark,
sawing and measuring and hammering as if there was no tomorrow.

The blue sky turned grey and the grey, black,
and finally the ark was completed.
As storm clouds gathered above
all the creatures gathered too.
Elephants came, swinging their trunks.
Behind them waddled two skunks.
Lions pranced, striking a pose.
And squirrels hopped in, holding their nose!
The fishes of the sea came swimming up to the ark.
The birds of the air flew down to it.
And pretty soon there were two of each, a male and a female, of
	every size, shape and kind of living creature that lived on
	Earth.
Even bacteria came.
No one recognized them, so they came in hiding, inside the bodies
	of the other animals.
As for the Noahs, they stood on the sidelines and watched,
counting all the creatures so that none would be left out for good.
Finally, after nearly a week, all of the creatures had gathered on the
	ark.

All of the creatures, that is, except one: the human being.
Mr. and Mrs. Noah, their three sons and their three wives, had not
     yet entered the ark.

2. The Great Debate on the Ark

It was not at all decided by the creatures of the Earth whether
     human beings should be allowed onto the ark.
Even though the Noah family had worked so hard to build the ark
many creatures felt that there was no place in the world for humans.
There arose a heated debate among them,
so heated that the two polar bears couldn't take part.
They had to go down to the ice room to cool off.
At first, a few of the animals spoke out against letting humans on.
"Why should we let them on?" neighed the horse.
"They tie us up and drag us wherever it pleases them to go."
"Why should we let them on?" fluttered the butterfly.
"They smoke up the air and make it hard for us to flap our wings."
But some of the animals took the side of the humans.
"Aw," said the cockroach in a creepy voice, "let 'em on, will ya?
I like the way they scream and jump, scream and jump, to get outta
     my way."
"Aw," said the spider in a whisper, "let 'em on, will ya?
I like the way they build spooky attics and cellars for my webs."
Before long, there was great commotion and a lot of loud shouting
     on the ark.
For the animals were split right down the middle, half in favor, half
     against:
To make room or not to make room. *That* was the question!

And the hours rolled by … and the skies grew even darker …
darker than the blackest night …
and the clouds rumbled a million drums …
"It won't be long. IT WON'T BE LONG!!!"

Finally, the hippo's wife climbed onto her husband's back so that she
        could be seen by all the animals.
"Silence, everyone!" she hollered, opening her mouth as wide as a
        canyon.
"We will take a vote.
All those in favor of letting humans on the ark raise your … well,
        your … well, raise something.
All those against, lower something
or just lie down on your bellies or whatever you have that resembles
        a belly."
The pigs stuck up their snouts
and the rabbits raised their rumps.
The deer upped their antlers
and the camels hiked their humps.
But the sharks flumped their fins
and the bears bounced down on their belly.
While the cats tilted their tails
and the rhinos' horns turned to jelly!
The kangaroos and the gnus
The bees and the fleas
The monkeys and the donkeys …
All voted "No."
But the bats and the rats
The slugs and the bugs

The crocs and one fox
All voted "Yes."
(The other fox abstained.)
All for their own reasons.
The bacteria didn't vote,
because no one knew they were there in the first place.
Meanwhile, the Noahs, their three sons and their three wives,
waited anxiously outside the big door of the ark.
They were biting their nails, a thing that definitely puzzled the
     animals.
With the storm upon them
and the creatures still bitterly divided,
Noah stood tall at the door of the ark and said …
"We are one of you."
To this his wife, standing shoulder to shoulder with him, added …
"We wish to create a better world someday for all creatures, big and
     small."

Lightning crashed, thunder roared,
and water began to pour from the sky
as if a bottomless ocean had been turned upside down.
And suddenly all of the creatures,
seeing the terrible storm,
stood up, or flew up, or flapped around as best they could inside the
     ark.
They all felt sorry for the Noah family and didn't want to see them
     die.
And they remembered, most of all,
that the Noahs, their three sons and their three wives,
were good human beings who had done

whatever was humanly possible
to save all the creatures under the sun.

And that is how human beings were saved from the flood
after the Great Debate on the Ark.

3. The Flood and the Rainbow

The rains lasted for forty days and forty nights.
The waters rose and rose
until a vast ocean covered the face of Earth.
Even the tallest peaks of the tallest mountains didn't so much as
        peek out of the water.
It was as if the air itself was being smothered between sea and sky.
It rained and it rained …
it rained and it rained some more …
until all that was left was a planet of water
with Noah's Ark bobbing up and down on it.

Meanwhile, inside the ark, none of the creatures, who now included
        the Noah family,
knew what on earth their fate would be.
Even the snake, who was used to scaring the wits out of other
        creatures,
shuddered until it almost lost its skin.
Even the leopard, who was used to scaring the life out of other
        creatures,
shivered until its spots became all blurry.
Even the tiger, who was used to scaring the daylights out of other

creatures,
shook until its stripes scrambled like runny eggs.
And even the elephant, so big and brave, hid behind the mouse,
though this didn't make him the least bit invisible.
Finally, the female dove flew to the very top rafter of the ceiling.
"Hear me!" she called to all.
"I will fly over the waters to see what I can see."
All of the creatures praised the dove's lofty words.
And the dove flew out the open window of the ark to see what she
          could see.
The creatures waited and waited, fearing for their future.
Toward evening the dove came back.
But she had nothing to show for herself.
"What did you see?" asked the goat.
"Water, water, nothing but water," answered the dove.
"Not even some nice hot desert between the water?"
asked the lizard, licking her nostrils.
"Water, water, nothing but water," repeated the dove.
"Wasn't there even a tiny patch of dry land anywhere?"
asked Noah, scratching his long white beard.
"Nowhere to be seen," replied the dove.
"But we must build houses for our grandchildren and their
          children's children."
There was nothing more that the dove could say.
But nonetheless she flew out the next day
and the next day, day after day
until one day, she returned to the ark
with the twig of an olive tree in her beak.
And all the creatures knew in an instant that she had found land.
Land where green trees grow.
Land where fresh breezes blow.

Land where rivers run and blossoms bloom.
Land for me and land for you.
And the sun, hidden for so long, pitched a rainbow high up in the sky,
and all of the creatures looked there,
and they knew that they were saved
… for now if not forever.

4. What Comes Now?

As the waters ebbed under a blazing sun
the ark came to rest on the peak of a tall mountain.
Two by two the creatures left the ark,
some by land and some by sea
and some in the air that made them free.
They were all so happy to have their only home again,
the earth beneath their feet
and the sea, a place to live.
As for the Noahs,
they were the very last creatures to leave the ark.

And as Noah watched all the other creatures walk, swim or fly away,
he looked up into the sky once more.
The beautiful rainbow was still there, radiant
for all the world to see.
Noah smiled.
His bones weren't shivering inside his body,
and he thought to himself …
"Finally we humans are at one with the world."
But before the creatures said their sad goodbyes,

they formed a circle under the rainbow,
some on land, some in the sea,
and some in the air that made them free.
And they sang or whistled or hummed or gurgled this song:

> We have survived
> But what comes now?
> We are alive
> Do we know how
> To save the Earth?
> Let's make a vow
> Here and now!

As they sang this, the rainbow flashed,
burning the sky with the light of a thousand suns,
before disappearing into thin air.
And on that spot,
as time passed history by,
the ark fell to pieces and vanished, leaving no trace of itself.

And all the creatures,
including Noah, his wife, their three sons and their three wives,
went their own way
covering the face of Earth.

THE TOWER OF BABEL

1. In the Beginning

Once upon a time there was an enormous and beautiful tower.
How tall was it? Well, I'll tell you.
It reached so tall into the sky that clouds gathered around it like
     cotton.
It rocketed so high that no birds could ever fly to the top to build a
     nest.
The few that tried got exhausted, fell back to Earth and promptly
     died.
In short, the tower was so tall that nobody knew how really tall it was.

This tower was called The Tower of Babel.

Now, you may be wondering how it came to be built in the first place
and what happened to it in the end.
Well, in the beginning, all people spoke the same language.
They lived in peace and harmony with each other.
They understood what was in each other's heart.
But some among them imagined themselves living far above the
     ground.
They wanted to be taller than other people, greater than nature itself.
They envisioned a tower that reached to the heavens
and a city surrounding it below.
"We will build a tower that towers over all the land," they said.

"We will become so powerful
that nothing from the outside will ever destroy us."
And filled with pride and the love of greed, they set to work,
to build a tower that could be seen and feared by all.
They worked like the devil, felling tree after tree.
They toiled day and night, turning mountains into dust.
They labored without rest, leveling the land.
There were men hauling rocks half the size of the sky.
There were women bearing sand in long lines, like ants.
Even the children were not spared.
They helped bake the bricks that were used for the walls.

So …
day by day
week upon week
month after month
the tower rose before their eyes.
And even before it could be completed
the people started to fight and rush into it.
They pushed and shoved, pulled and tugged, all trying to be first.
No one would let anyone else stay on the floor they called their own.

2. The Wars of Misunderstanding

Eventually people settled on all the floors of The Tower of Babel.
They lived in big groups that they formed on their floors.
While they met from time to time on the stairs to chat, argue and
        trade,
they kept mostly to their floor.

Over time, the people on one floor knew less and less about the
people on another.
People tried, as best as they could, to ignore anyone living on the
floors above or below them.
They did this quite well, except when there was some noise or
disturbance.

For instance, to give you an idea,
the people who lived on the 302nd floor celebrated June 11 as their
"Floor Day."
But the people on the 303rd floor considered June 11 *their* "Floor
Day" too.
Old 303rd Floorers told young 303rd Floorers that long ago in their
hazy past, on June 11, some people from the 302nd floor
came bounding up the stairs
claiming part of the 303rd floor as their own.
A savage war was fought.
Nobody won that war, but nobody lost it either.
Both floors declared victory on June 11.

Actually, no one really knows what happened on that blood-spilling
day
in June of the distant past.
But that doesn't matter when it comes to "Floor Days."
In history, it's not the event that counts but how it's celebrated a long
time later.

From the outside The Tower of Babel looked very peaceful,
impressive and spectacular.
But on the inside things were a total mess.

Now, there is one thing that you absolutely must know about this tower.

Each floor had developed its own language.

This made it very hard for people to communicate from floor to floor.

For instance, one day a man from the 701st floor climbed a floor and said …

"SMIRGY MUF BA DOOGLE."

This meant …

"We would appreciate it if you wouldn't dance in the middle of the night."

Luckily, a woman on the 702nd floor spoke the man's language.

She had once been an exchange student to the 701st floor.

So she said …

"BOKA BOKA NU. GORDY HAPA KU!"

This meant …

"It's our young people. They like to dance late at night. Please put up with it. We do."

But this sort of thing happened too …

One day, way way down on the 8th floor, an important meeting took place.

After the meeting, the 8th Floorers sent a delegation down to the 6th floor.

"JADAJADAGRIMSUPPUI!" said the head of the 8th-Floor delegation.

This meant …

"We want to join with you and take over the 7th floor!"

But, thank goodness, the 6th Floorers were a peaceful and happy

people, and they replied …
"HOGAH HOGAH! BOKULA BEGUMBY SA!"
This meant …
"Go back, go back! We don't want any of your warlike plans!"
Unfortunately, none of the 8th Floorers spoke 6th Floor.
They returned to their floor thinking that the 6th Floorers wanted to
　　　fight alongside them.

This is just a small sample of the thousands upon thousands of
　　　problems,
not to mention violent misunderstandings,
that you could witness inside The Tower of Babel.

3.　The Floorless People

There were people living in The Tower of Babel who did not have a
　　　floor of their own.
They were called "The Floorless."

The people living on the 697th floor were very unhappy and poor.
They didn't have enough water to stay alive.
"It's those awful people on the 696th floor," hollered one man,
　　　standing on a table and waving his arms in the air.
"They are stopping our flow of water."
"No," cried a young woman. "It's the fault of our own leaders.
They are keeping our water for themselves alone."
"That's not the problem," said an old man.
"It's the young people of our floor.
They waste water like there was no tomorrow."

So you see, even when people speak the same language, there is no
       guarantee that they understand each other.

After that, I am sad to have to tell you,
the people on the 697th floor started to fight among themselves.
Furniture and lights were smashed.
Doors and walls were broken down.
Bedrooms were entered with the most violent consequences.
Water pipes were cut, like veins.
Finally the stronger people took over the floor.
They chased those who had opposed them away.
Those weaker people chased away had nowhere to go.
They became "The Floorless."

These Floorless moved up and down the tower.
But no one on the floors above or below would take them in.
They were told that there wasn't enough room for them on any floor.
They were told that there wasn't enough money for them on any
       floor.
They were told that no one could understand them on any floor.

So the Floorless could only go lower and lower,
or higher and higher,
living out their lives in between floors.
"How high must we go?" one child asked.
She was so skinny and frail that she barely had enough breath in her
       to climb another stair.
"Just a little higher," said her mother, with tears in her eyes.
And, shivering from the bitterest cold,
the mother wrapped her stick-like arms around her child.

Sometimes people came out onto the stairs to give them
a blanket
or a coin
or a morsel of food.
But they never gave them the hope that someday
they would be taken in and comforted.

The fate of these poor Floorless People was
to climb down The Tower of Babel as it descended to the surface of
        the Earth …
and to climb up The Tower of Babel as it scraped the floor of heaven.

4. The Fate of the Tower of Babel

Let me tell you what happened to The Tower of Babel in the end.

The Tower of Babel wasn't built in a day, or a year, or a century
or even in a thousand thousand years.
But it was brought down before anyone could stop it
in the blink of time's eye.
And it was destroyed from the top, the bottom and the middle alike.

You see, there were a few people on each floor who spoke the
        languages
and knew the hearts of people on other floors.
But sadly no one listened to them.
"WAMANAKI LUZU LUZU … I speak many languages," said an
        old and wise woman.

"I will travel through the floors and tell everyone not to fight."
"TOSEMUNGA BABAI! … Stop her!" yelled a woman whose
    brother had once disappeared on another floor.
"She is a traitor to our floor!"
"Let's make big holes in our floor's floor and drown everyone
    below!"
"Good idea!"
"Let's set fire to our ceiling and burn the next floor's floor!"
"Good idea!"
"Those people above us are stupid. They don't even understand our
    language."
"Those people below us are stupid. They don't even understand our
    language."
"Those people above us are evil. They want to take over our floor."
"Those people below us are evil. They want to take over our floor."

On every floor
up and down
above and below
from the top of the Earth to the bottom of the sky
these were the words heard inside The Tower of Babel.
And they were heard in every single language.

And the funny thing is,
even though these words were said in different languages,
they were exactly the same words.
And the even funnier thing is,
almost no one on any floor knew that they were saying the exact
    same things as everyone else …
and those who knew were silenced.

Silence, too, sounds the same in all languages.

So, floor by floor, The Tower of Babel was brought down.
It was brought down by people saying the same things without
        knowing it.

And what happened then?
The Tower of Babel became nothing more than a mountain of ugly
        stone,
a great towering ruin
rubble
good for nothing on Earth.

The people who were still alive, from all the floors and all the stairs
found themselves together on the ground again,
walking away from each other
dispersing
wandering
from place to place
and land to land.
Even now they could not live with each other,
even now, standing tall and equal on their own two feet.

"After all, even though we are all human beings,
we don't speak the same language, *do* we."
That's what they all said … in their own language, of course.

As for The Tower of Babel,
in time
no one remembered it.

No one but you, that is.

GUCHA GOO (The End)

DAVID AND GOLIATH

1. An Era Like Any Other

It appeared to be an era like any other.
No sooner was one war over than someone was starting another
    one.
People had stopped using the words "after the war"
gradually replacing them with the words "between wars."
You couldn't be blamed for thinking that people at that time
loved nothing more than to be at each other's throats.
And what did they do when they were at each other's throats?
Did they talk with each other in gentle voices?
(After all, there is no need to shout when you are throat to throat
    with another person.)
Did they stretch out a palm and stroke each other's cheeks?
(After all, it doesn't take much effort to open a palm.)
Did they close their eyes in trust?
No.
They shouted and screamed
ranted and raved
raised hands in the air
and made sure that they never, never, never took eyes off of each
    other
not even for a split second.
Even "between wars," people acted much like they did "during
    wars."

"We must never let down our guard,"
cried the leaders of all of the nations that existed at that time.
"If we do, we might be attacked.
People who are our between-war friends may turn against us."

So, as time rushed by from war to war,
the people of all of the nations adopted symbols
just in case their between-war friends turned against them.
One nation adopted the symbol of the human hand clasped around
      a very ugly man's throat.
(The definition of "ugly" in those days was "not looking like your
      own people.")
Another nation's symbol was two enormous swords embedded in
      the temples of a beast.
(The facial features of this "beast" happened to resemble those of the
      people who lived in a neighboring nation.)
Yet another symbol adopted by a nation was two huge perfectly
      round googly eyes.
Under them was written: "There is no escape from us!"
Apparently those eyes were directed not only at the people of other
      nations,
but also at the people of the nation adopting that symbol.
So, you see, no one could be trusted in those days, not even yourself.

But there was one person who was different from all others.
His name was David.
David was a thin and soft-spoken young man, a shepherd,
as mild as he was shy.
He was the youngest of eight children.
His father, whose name was Saul, was fondest of him among all of

his children.
"I could not live if something happened to you," he said.
"Though we are now about to end another between-war period by
        entering into a war,
you must look after yourself.
You were not born to fight like all the others."
It was true.
Just about everybody loved to fight in those days.
All you had to do was gather people together in groups and show
        them
a hand strangling a neck or
a sword piercing through a head or
two huge perfectly round googly eyes
and they would drop whatever they were doing,
baking bread
making beds
sailing ships
or kissing lips
and rush out to drench their former friends in a shower of blood.

Yes, it certainly was an era like any other.

2. Concerts by the River

Except for David.
He rarely spoke to anybody, not even his sheep.
When people gathered to hear the speeches of their leaders,
David went the other way.
He took his sheep far up the slope of the mountain.

He stopped by the river, his favorite spot in all the world,
and played his lyre for the sheep.
Now, sheep are not particularly known for their sensitivity to the
        sounds of the lyre,
or any other string instrument, for that matter.
But when David played, they sat down in rows
all the way up the slope of the mountain
and gave him their undivided attention.
If a lamb would start to nod off, especially in the summer when the
        warm breezes blew,
its mother would nudge it awake and scowl …
"Don't you fall asleep when David is playing his lyre.
Who do you think he's playing for anyway? It's for us."
After each concert by the river on the slope of the mountain,
the sheep would bleat in unison.
If a lamb failed to bleat, distracted, say, by a hawk flying above,
its father would give it a little kick in the side.
These concerts took place every day, like clockwork.
They were so regular that the sheep, setting eyes on the river,
would rush up the slope of the mountain
to get the best seats for themselves and their lambs.
But if David caught even one sheep butting another sheep out of a
        seat,
he canceled that day's music.
This kept the sheep better in line than raising the staff.
The staff was the instrument of choice for all other shepherds in the
        land.
But not for David.
He had his lyre.

One day, not long after David had finished playing the lyre for his
	flock,
when the sheep were dozing by the river under a peach-yellow sun,
Saul came trudging up the slope of the mountain with an expression
	of grave worry on his face.
He sat down on a large flat rock beside his son and said …
"David. I have something that I want you to do for me."
David smiled at his father without saying a word, a hand resting on
	his lyre.
"Three of your brothers have gone off to fight our between-war
	friends."
("Between-war friend" had become the word for enemy.)
"One of them is the most powerful man on Earth.
His name is Goliath.
No one can rid the world of this man.
He alone controls everything through power and the fear of its use.
His people bask in his shadow.
Nothing seems impossible to them when they stand behind Goliath.
But now those people have become too proud.
They lord themselves over everyone else.
Your brothers are very brave.
They are risking their lives in order to stop this one man from
	taking over all the nations.
I want you to take them food from home.
But you must not fight!
When they see their little brother, frail and helpless,
they will feel a great strength growing inside them.
It will give them courage to stand up to the dreaded Goliath."

3. David's Journey to the Field of Battle

So David set out from his home with grain for bread and ten
    cheeses.
He did not forget to take his lyre with him, strapped to his back.
He was lost without it.

Many people saw David plodding along the rough paths toward the
    field of battle.
Some knew of his skill with the lyre and begged him to stop and
    play.
But David said to them …
"I will play my lyre when I am face to face with Goliath.
If you want to hear it, come and follow me."
And, what do you know? They dropped what they were doing
filling pails
raising quails
tilling soil
and measuring oil.
They took whatever meager food they had in their homes at the time
and followed behind David
as he made his way along the rough paths toward the field of battle.

"Please, please," they entreated him time and time again,
"just play us one song on your lyre. For we are tired, and it will give
    us comfort."
But David refused to play.
Even at night, when they all rested in the clearing of a cedar grove,

when the transparent strains of his music would have flown straight
        up to the sky,
its notes, a thousand bees, pollinating stars …
even then, David would not play.
Finally, all of the people fell asleep without a care for themselves
and they dreamt of a time when former enemies would truly be
        friends
and friends, friends for life.

David, bearing the grain for bread and the ten cheeses,
his lyre strapped tightly to his back, arrived at the camp,
followed by the many people who had brought food from home
to give strength to their people.
"Where are my three brothers?" he asked a man dressed in a suit of
        shiny bronze armor.
"I have brought food from home for them."
"Your brothers are on top of that ridge," he said, pointing into the
        distance.
"They are very brave, but there is nothing that we can do against
        Goliath.
The world has never seen a man as all-powerful."
"We have no choice but to be his slaves," shouted another man
        nearby,
shedding his armor and flinging it to the ground.
"No force is strong enough to save us. We are doomed."
And the man promptly plopped down on top of his armor, weeping.
"Where is my brothers' tent?" asked David.
"It is over there, by the river," said the man in shiny bronze armor,
sticking a finger inside his mail and scratching his belly.
So David went to his brothers' tent.

He put the grain and the ten cheeses on a roughly hewn bench
        outside it,
then walked to the river and knelt by its edge.
He took a long drink of water from it in his cupped hands.
The water was cold and clear,
and it reminded him of the water in the river up the slope of the
        mountain,
and he thought of his home and his father and his sheep.
But, instead of crying he took a very deep breath,
stood up and walked directly up the hill alone
to the very top of the ridge.

4. The Challenge

No sooner did David's three brothers see him approach than they
        hollered at him with great ferocity …
"What on earth are you doing here?!"
"Go back, go home! You don't belong here!"
"You must stay away from here! We can die,
but you of all people must survive for everyone."
Though they were fearless when it came to themselves,
they feared in their bones for David's life.

That was when it came …
a deafening thump, as if thunder was echoing straight across the
        valley.
And then another thump, as ear splitting as the one before.
They all looked to the ridge across the valley
and they saw him …

Goliath, a mammoth of a man, stomping his feet against the stony
　　cliff.
And every time he stomped, the men from his nation standing by
　　him
(who only came up to his belly button at the very highest)
called out in the direction of the ridge
where David and his three elder brothers were.
BOOM! "You will be destroyed, so surrender now!"
BOOM! "Drop your swords, if you know what's good for you!"
BOOM! "Give up, and you can eventually be like us!"
And Goliath, with a bronze helmet on his head so heavy that it would
　　have crushed the head of any other man to the size of an acorn,
and with a coat of mail so massive that you could have fit ten normal
　　men inside it and still had enough room to play a game of
　　checkers …
this monster of a man, Goliath
raised his arms far into the air and shouted at the top of his lungs …
"Choose a man to fight me, any man.
If he fights and kills me,
then all my people will surrender to you.
But if he fights and I kill him,
then all of your people will live in peace under US!"
Again he thumped his colossal feet against the stones of the cliff.
The men around him, who were now putting on faces so fierce that
　　not even their mothers would have recognized them, screamed
　　out …
BOOM! "There is no one who can face Goliath!"
BOOM! "There is no one who can beat Goliath!"
BOOM! "GOLIATH!" BOOM! "GOLIATH!" BOOM! BOOM!
　　BOOOOOM!

Then, out of the blue, David started down the hill toward the river.
He wanted to say something to Goliath.
Yet he knew that his voice was too soft and far too meek to reach
        across the valley to the opposite ridge.
As he walked, his three elder brothers called to him …
"Stop, David!"
"David, where are you going?"
"David, David, that valley is no place for a person like you!"
From the other ridge came only raucous laughter and jeers.
"Oh, look at the little boy, the little weakling!"
"They are not men, they are cowards, forcing their children to die
        for them!"
"Hey, watch out for the lyre. He could hit us on the head with it!"
Goliath seemed to especially fancy this last comment.
He slapped his sides and laughed so loud that five men on either side
        of him were bowled off their feet by the sound.

When David reached the bottom of the valley, he stopped.
He took the lyre off of his back and looked up at Goliath and his
        men.
The setting sun hung in the sky, eclipsed by Goliath's head.
"Hear me, Goliath," said David in a soft flutey voice.
"Your head is now eclipsing the sun.
You are the moon.
But I am the Earth.
It is you who will be moved by my weight.
You will sink below the horizon.
But, unlike the moon, you will vanish from the heavens.
You who could have been the sun itself
now block the light of the sun from me, the Earth!"

And as David played his lyre, the strains of his music swarmed up
        the hill and over the ridge
into the air and far far up to the sky,
nudging the sun
until its slivered light flashed
across and along the deep valley.

5. Goliath's End

Now, with the sun hanging low over the ridge
and Goliath casting a shadow from there to the ends of the Earth,
David stopped playing his music and spoke.
"I will fight you. Come down to this valley.
Meet me on my own ground."
And as he spoke, again there were jeers from the ridge in front of
        him,
and shudders from the ridge behind.
Goliath made his way down the hill, step by giant step.
David knelt by the river.
The cold clear water reminded him of his home.
He picked up a smooth stone from the riverbed and rubbed it in his
        palms.
Then he took a sling from his pocket, the very same sling that he had
        used to drive lions and bears from his sheep,
and placed the stone carefully in it.
By then Goliath, whose vision was sharper than that of an eagle,
who missed nothing that happened near him or faraway,
had arrived on the opposite bank of the river.
He planted his feet on the ground and said to David …

"Do you really think that you, a weak boy, can take on Goliath with
        your little boy's toy?
Are your people so cowardly that they send children to fight men?
If so, then you all deserve to die!
I do not want to kill you, little boy.
But if you pretend not to fear me, it is the only course open to me."
"I pretend nothing, Goliath, certainly not fear," said David.
"Everyone speaks of your great strength.
It is something that the world can see as clear as day.
But you have chosen to use that strength to bring the terror of death
to the people of other lands.
I, David, will stop you!"
Hearing this, Goliath raised his right arm high in the air,
then, bringing it down, drew his mighty sword from its scabbard.
The raised blade was so thick and long and sharp that it sliced the
        sky above the valley in two.
"I am sorry for you and your people," said Goliath, about to step
        over the river and sever David's head from his shoulders in
        one fell swoop.
"No," said David, twirling the sling above his head.
"I am sorry for you and your people.
Your strength is your weakness …
your bravery, your bane."

And, as the sun rolled along its path, now split by the cliff's edge,
David let fly his stone.
It sailed through the air spinning and whirring,
striking Goliath in the very center of his forehead.
Goliath stood perfectly still.
The sun dropped below the ridge.

The first stars, twinkling, tracked up the tilted sky.
And, all along, Goliath stood where he was, perfectly erect,
only the point of his raised sword catching that day's final light.
And none of the men there,
on the ridge in front of David or the ridge behind him,
knew whether Goliath was alive or dead.
All they knew is that he had been stopped in his tracks by a soft-
       spoken young man named David.

Finally, when complete darkness fell, so did Goliath.
He made no sound when he hit the Earth.
The river's water carried Goliath away from there,
as if he had no weight at all.

As for David, he left his lyre on the spot where Goliath had stood.
And, without looking up to either ridge,
with his head bowed and eyes fixed in front of him,
he followed the river all the way home.

SAMSON AND DELILAH

1. The Lion in the Vineyard

There once was a man so strong that no man or woman could resist
    him.
Even as a little boy his strength was in evidence.
He didn't like the breakfast gruel that his mother gave him,
so he hurled the bowl straight up into the air.
Samson and his mother waited and waited for it to come down.
The sun rose to the zenith and the sun set.
The stars came out and dawn eventually broke.
Two days later, around noon, the bowl came dropping out of the sky,
landing on the very spot where Samson had refused to eat his gruel.
The bowl shattered into dust, leaving a crater in the middle of the
    garden.
That happened when Samson was seven.
And he was utterly stubborn to boot.
Once Samson made up his mind about something,
a team of wild elephants couldn't alter his course.
Even his parents held little sway over him.
But they loved him nevertheless,
for he was their son and heir.
The tales of his miraculous feats of strength
were known throughout the land.
"Samson is the strongest man in the world," said a woman, visiting
    his parents.

"Well, maybe one of the strongest," replied his mother in all
      modesty.
"Ridiculous," cried his father. "My son could beat any man's son.
      Just let 'em try!"
It was usual in those days for young boys to brag about the prowess
      of their fathers,
but not many fathers made such claims for their son.
Then again, not many sons could send a bowl of gruel into the air for
      two days,
not, at least, at age seven.

Samson grew up to be a very handsome man,
and the time came for him to take a wife.
Actually, Samson had already been toying with this idea for some
      time
and trying it on with any number of women.
One day he went to his parents and said …
"Mother, father, I have chosen the woman I want to marry."
"That's wonderful, dear," said his mother. "Do we know the lucky
      girl?"
"Well, not really."
"Then introduce us quickly," said his father. "Is she from the
      neighborhood?"
"Well, not really."
"Then where does she live?" asked his mother.
"Actually, she is not one of us."
"Not one of us?" said his mother, grimacing as if the juice of ten
      lemons had been poured between her lips.
"No."
"Then who is she one of?" asked his father, shaking his head.

"Actually, she is the daughter of a people who are our enemy."
Samson's parents immediately began to rant and rave,
forbidding him from taking a wife from among the enemy.
But Samson was determined,
and once Samson was determined
no person alive could deflect him from his course.

Samson decided to tell his parents how he had met his bride.
He had been traveling through her land,
when he came upon vineyards at harvest time.
The clouds in the sky were like pillows on a bed of blue.
Samson caught sight of the beautiful young woman picking grapes.
She slipped a grape into her mouth and held it for a moment
        between her teeth.
He was instantly entranced by her beauty
by the redness of her lips
the fullness of her hips
and skin as soft and smooth as the pillow-like clouds.
But just as Samson was about to approach her,
a lion appeared from out of nowhere.
It rushed straight toward him and leapt onto him.
The lion could not know that he had his match in Samson,
who grabbed the fierce beast by its shaggy mane
and cast it summarily to the ground.
The lion, flat on its back, emitted a thin whimper,
thrust its four legs rigidly into the air,
and promptly expired.
The young woman standing by the vines was rather impressed.
Swallowing her grape, she smiled generously at Samson.
Samson left the vineyard,

promising to return to make the young woman his wife.
He told the story of how he met her faithfully to his parents,
leaving out the minor detail of how he had killed the lion.
Samson's parents always became distressed when hearing of his
        exploits,
and he didn't want to worry them any more than necessary.

That is how Samson met his first wife,
after killing the lion that might have come between them.

2. Late-Picked Grapes

Samson's parents were none too pleased about their son's choice of a
        wife.
But Samson did whatever his fancy dictated,
and only woe came to the person who attempted to defy Samson's
        fancy.
Samson returned to the land of the woman who was to be his bride,
finding her again picking grapes for the harvest.
"Late-picked grapes are the sweetest of all," she said to him.
And the two of them laid down beside the spot where the lion had
        been killed,
where now a dense swarm of bees swirled up in a pillar.
A pool of thick honey spread slowly over the ground.
Samson and his bride-to-be rolled in this honey
until every pore of their bodies could feel sweetness seeping in.
The pillar of bees covered Samson's back,
and the bees, in a frenzy of buzzing, stung him savagely.
But Samson was oblivious to the piercing pain,

and the bees, their one sting in life gone,
dropped aside and were still.
Then Samson helped his bride-to-be up,
and the two of them stood naked among the vines,
as a downpour of cool rain fell over them,
washing the last remnants of honey from their bodies.
When Samson told his parents about how he came to take his wife,
he left out the part about the bees and the honey.
There were some things that parents in those days found hard to
        listen to.

Now, the people that Samson's wife belonged to were not well
        disposed toward Samson.
They treated both him and his wife with disdain,
particularly the wife, who was seen as a traitor to their causes.
They hatched a plot to find out secrets that would help them in their
        wars,
and insisted that she be a part of them.
For seven days and seven nights she pressed Samson
for him to divulge secrets that would help her people in their wars.
But Samson, more wily than his massive muscles might suggest,
read through her entreaties
and set about to kill thirty of her people,
which he did with such swiftness
that they were dead before they knew it.

When his wife's father learned of this,
he forced his daughter to leave Samson,
and, out of spite, gave her to a good friend of Samson,
a friend who had been the best man at his wedding.

When Samson learned of this, he reacted rather badly.
He went out and caught three hundred foxes.
He then made one hundred and fifty torches.
He turned the foxes tail to tail and tied the torches to them.
He set fire to the torches,
releasing them in the grain fields and the olive orchards of the
        enemy.
He spared the vineyards,
for he still had a soft spot for his beautiful wife
and for the place where they had bathed themselves in honey.

After that, Samson went up into the high rocks of the mountains
from which he watched the fires on the plain burn
flare
and turn to cinder and cold ash.

3. The Temple and the Pond

There was no end to the feats of Samson.
Soldiers from other nations came in great number to his haven in
        the mountains, saying to him …
"Samson. We will bind you and take you down the mountain."
"Swear to me," said Samson, "that you will not kill me yourselves."
"We promise you. We will only deliver you to your enemies,
who are our masters.
We will not kill you ourselves."
They tied him with two new ropes and delivered him into the hands
        of his enemy.
But no sooner was he delivered there than did he snap the ropes like
        threads,

and, picking up the jawbone of an ass that happened to be lying
        there,
went on to kill each and every one of a thousand men.
After that, standing in the doorway of the enemy's temple,
he pushed down the pillars that were holding it up for good
        measure,
bringing the building down with an Earth-shattering crash.
And when he was finished he was tired and thirsty,
for even Samson got tired and thirsty from killing a thousand men
        with the jawbone of an ass
and bringing a temple down, for good measure.
He knelt by the side of a large pond and drank long from it.
In fact, he drank so long that there was no water left in the pond
        when he was finished.
And, with hundreds of little fish flopping about on the muddy
        bottom,
Samson proceeded to pee, for he had taken into his body much
        water.
Gradually the pond filled up again,
and the little fish started to swim about in it as before.
To this day,
the fish in what came to be known as "The Waters of Samson Pond"
possess a slightly bitter, salty taste beloved by the people of that
        region.

4. The Death of Samson

It wasn't long before Samson fell head over heels in love with
        another woman.

This woman was the most beautiful of all that he had ever laid eyes
       on.
Her name was Delilah, and he married her.
By now, everybody in the world
(such as the world was known to be at that time)
desired to learn the source of Samson's great strength.
Only Samson knew the secret,
and he wasn't about to tell anybody,
not his parents and not his friends,
and not even Delilah, who he gladly told everything else.

Samson's enemies came to her,
offering her more money than she could dream of,
if only she would tell them how to bring about Samson's death.
That night Delilah pressed herself against Samson, saying to him …
"If you love me you will tell me
how you can be subdued."
And Samson naturally said to her …
"You are the only one who can subdue me, Delilah."
He wrapped his legs and arms tightly around her.
Not being able to move any part of her body except for her toes and
       mouth,
she wiggled her toes and said …
"I don't mean that. Tell me the secret of your strength, Samson."
Samson let go of her.
"If I am tied up with seven bowstrings that have not been dried,
I will not be able to break away."
The next night she bound Samson with seven bowstrings that had
       not been dried
and the enemies hurried into the room and pounced on him in his
       bed.

But Samson tore the bowstrings with a bare flex of his muscles,
making short shrift of the enemy before Delilah's very own eyes.
"You have lied to me," said Delilah. "You do not love me."
"I do love you, Delilah. That is why I have kept the secret to myself."
"No, you do not love me. You do not. You do not!"
Delilah started to weep a fountain of tears.
So convincing was her weeping that she all but believed in it herself.
"Well then," said Samson, once again enveloping her in his legs and
     arms,
"I will tell you. If the locks of my hair are woven together and
     pinned up,
I will be powerless against the most feeble foe."
So, the next night, once Samson was safely asleep,
Delilah wove the locks of his hair together and pinned them up.
Even she had to admit this made Samson look rather weak.
Once again his enemies hurried in and pounced on him in his bed.
But Samson, undoing his hair with one hand, put an end to his
     attackers with the other.
Then Delilah, who was standing dumbstruck in the corner, said …
"You have lied to me again. You do not love me. You do not. You
     do not!"
And she now cried such a sea of tears that Samson had to lay the
     bedcovers at her feet
lest the tears seep through cracks between the floorboards and flood
     the people below.

When the next night came, Delilah laid herself atop Samson.
Her skin was like fire, his like wax.
He burned inside with an indescribable desire.
"Tell me," she whispered into his ear.

"What is the true secret of your strength?
If you love me you will tell me."
And after the fire inside him flared and cooled to a wisp of smoke,
he laid his head in her naked lap and said to her …
"The hair on my head has never been cut, not since birth.
If it is cut from my head, I will lose all of my strength."

Samson fell into a deep sleep in Delilah's lap.
She called in men who were waiting outside the room.
One of them cut all the locks of hair from Samson's head
as Delilah held his head up in front of her naked breasts.
When the razor that cut Samson's hair was put down,
the enemies threw themselves on Samson.
Samson, now half awake and as powerless as the next man,
was subdued with chains of bronze and led away.
Delilah remained unmoved in the middle of the bed,
her skin covered in a blanket of hair.

Samson was kept in prison.
He was abused and taunted,
tortured and ridiculed,
no one noticing, in their obsessive amusement,
that the hair on his head was growing back.

One sunny day, the leader of the enemy said …
"Stand Samson between the pillars of our great house
so that we may remember this giant reduced to a mouse."
The other leaders and their many followers cheered from the
        balconies and windows of the great house.
"Samson Between the Pillars!" they shouted.

"Samson Between the Bars!"
"Samson a Razed Mountain!"
"Samson … a Fallen Star!"

They mocked him with jeers.
They reviled him with obscenities.
They could not contain their derision.
Delilah, her body dripping with jewels, stood on the balcony above
        Samson, leading the chorus of indignity.
"Push, Samson, push the pillars!" they yelled.
"Pull, Samson, pull the pillars!"
"Once you were our monster!"
"Now you are our fool!"

Samson, shaking his full head of hair in the wind,
took hold of the two massive pillars of the great house.
He gripped one in each hand
and leaned forward, bowing his head.
With the locks of his hair flowing over his shoulders like water,
he brought down the great house
with all of the leaders and followers
who were mocking him from its balcony, windows and stairs.

Samson, too, was crushed to death,
as was Delilah, her flattened body still dripping with jewels,
together under a mound of pulverized stone.

Not long after that
his father and mother came to unearth their son's body.
They carried him home, his bones splintered inside him.

And, once home, they buried him
in the middle of their garden
where there had once been a crater
formed when a bowl
fell out of the sky
and was shattered to dust.

SUSANNA

1. The Prosecution

The judge's knuckled finger pointed straight to the top of the sky.
It was nearing noon
and the morning haze had long since burnt down,
leaving clouds that rested, a chain, on the horizon.

A table and four chairs had been set up in the town square.
Surrounding this public court was a dense circle of citizens,
each one cradling a deadly weapon in their hands:
fruit knives and jagged rocks
ropes, iron bars and pruning shears
bricks, hammers and carefully broken glass.
And there were many guns, too,
for it was the custom in this country to carry them freely
for security's sake, if for no other good reason.
The duty-bound members of the community,
strengthened in their circle,
followed the line up from the tip of the judge's finger,
seeing in the sky whatever they desired to see,
and taking from it the solace that they needed
to justify their role in what was to take place that sweltering day.

Sitting before the judge's table were the two prosecutors,
staunch and steadfast pillars of the community,

men held in high esteem by all for their wealth
and the position they derived from it.
In the fourth chair sat the accused, Susanna,
clad only in the coarse dark-blue robe given her by the court,
hands folded in her lap,
braids of jet-black hair hanging in front of her face,
peering down with squinted eyes
into the very roots of the Earth.

The judge finally brought his hand down, kneaded his lumpy elbow
        and proclaimed …
"It is time for the evidence to be given.
Tell all here the truth of what you witnessed in the walled garden."

The first elder stood laboriously, bowed deeply to the judge,
bowed somewhat less deeply to the multitude of armed good citizens
and told his story.
This is what he said:
"It had been for some time that my respected friend and I
(the second elder, though remaining seated, bowed to the judge and
        gathered citizens)
… that we had been dearly concerned about the accused, Susanna.
A woman of genuine virtue must be safeguarded by her community,
and who is better placed to offer this safety than upstanding superiors
        such as ourselves.
(The two elders simultaneously stroked their beards, smiling
        graciously left and right.)
On the day in question, we found ourselves in the garden of her
        husband's house.
Now, you may ask yourself how we came to be there in the first place.

(The two elders exchanged glances, nodding generously to each
     other.)
The wisdom of intuition urged us to admit ourselves.
This gift accompanies age in those who bear responsibility for a
     community,
particularly in those with the means to execute that responsibility
justly
selflessly
not to mention permanently.

"The accused, Susanna, was seemingly devoted to her husband,
and yet something in the movements of her body engendered
     suspicion.
She was too graceful, as to be willfully seductive,
too undulating, as to be deliberately provocative,
altogether too sweet
altogether too artless
altogether too endearing
altogether too bewitching …
Yes, BEWITCHING, I tell you!
(The two elders scanned the circle of citizens, rubbing their palms
     over their thighs, flexing their nostrils overflowing white with
     hairs, and wheezing through the gaps in their stained teeth
     rapidly, as if panting.
Susanna, for her part, remained exactly as she was before, not
     showing the faintest response to the words or gestures of her
     breathless prosecutors.)

"Ah, my friends, loyal citizens of our radiant community!
You may wish to imagine before you a Susanna the wounded deer.

You may hope to recognize a Susanna the proud lioness.
But, see her for what she is in the flesh:
Susanna the recoiling snake!
(This sent a hiss around the circle, with some of its members now
          clutching their weapons.)

"Once in the garden, we took refuge behind a single tree,
eager only to expose the accused, Susanna.
We saw her enter, followed by two faithful maids.
Susanna looked about her garden pleasurably.
It was a blistering day not unlike this one.
She then sent her maids to fetch soap and olive oil for a bath in the
          pond.
We know these to be her words because we overheard them clearly.
With the maids gone and the garden door securely locked by them,
the accused, Susanna … disrobed, slowly, garment by garment,
until she had nothing on her body at all.
Yes, her naked flesh was a pale, translucent brown,
like sand washed smooth by gentle waves,
as soft as the fleece of the black baby lamb.
Her neck was long, thin and strong, a Grecian column.
Her red lips barely open, like buds of the rose,
her feet delicate, toes curled in like shells,
her lithe limbs stretching into the air,
her entire sturdy body giving off a dark glow,
a young kumquat tree under a full moon …
and I tell you all!
She set herself down on the edge of that pond in the captivating
          manner of a woman intent upon luring … yes, luring a man.
Yes, yes, yes … there can be no doubt about this point.

The accused, Susanna, was shamelessly flaunting her wiles
merely by sitting there in that titillating and alluring manner!"
At this, the second elder wiped his brow and mouth with a silk
handkerchief, while the first elder approached Susanna and
laid a hand on her.
Susanna looked up at him and spoke her first words with clear
disdain.
"Get your hand off of my head!"
But the elder, nonetheless, left it there, continuing …
"The fact is, my good friends …
the fact is, the accused, Susanna, this woman, this slithering snake,
was about to shed her virtue, as she had her garments,
for no sooner had she begun to stroke her naked flesh with the cool
water of the pond than did a young man appear beside her.
He proceeded immediately to cast aside his clothing.
He grabbed her hungrily from behind.
He took her parts in his hands and fondled them.
The accused, my friends, the accused, Susanna, did not resist!
The fact is …
the fact is … I mean, the fact is … the accused, Susanna
lay down in the grass beside him, in the lurid grass!
Shamelessly offering herself to the young man!
Opening herself up to him in the most lewd and despicable manner
of a woman, I mean … a wo … wo … man …"
The elder was suddenly experiencing difficulties in both speech and
breathing.
He had been overcome by the potency of his own vivid descriptions.
Seeing this, the judge waved him down by brushing his fingers in
the air,
and, raising his right palm, commanded the second elder to finish

the story.
The first elder plopped down into his chair, holding his hand over
        his heart.
So the second stood and spoke.
This is what he said:

"Naturally, the sense of righteousness that comes with the territory
        of our possessions outraged us.
Without so much as a mutual nod we stepped from behind our tree,
        revealed ourselves and shouted …

'Get your hands off of that man, filthy woman!'
Shocked and no doubt awed by the rampant authority inherent in
        our voices,
the young man sprung to his feet and, clutching his clothes to his
        body, he fled,
a terrified animal,
leaping over the wall of the garden and disappearing from our sight.
Not possessing the agilities of youth, we could hardly pursue him.
It may be unfortunate that neither of us can identify him.
But, the identity of the man is not today's point.
The point here and now, as I am sure all good citizens will agree,
is the contemptible absence of any morality
in the woman
the accused
Susanna!
It grieves us to be her prosecutors,
as I know it grieves all of you
to see such a beautiful woman abuse eternal beauty for temporary
        lust.

But, my dear friends …
were grief to be justice's guide
the wicked would flower and the righteous, wither.
Sin would reign over the land in a guise of mercy,
and those who would pretend to a generosity of spirit
would lord over all men with a false and vindictive sympathy.
So you see, we were left no choice
but to take Susanna into our custody
and bring her here before you
so that her actions may be judged
in today's harsh light.
With this, I say to you all, my loyal friends …
we rest our case."

The second elder took his seat and shook hands with the first elder.
Both looked to the judge
for a swift verdict.
The accused, Susanna,
remained unmoved,
staring as before
into the roots of the Earth.

2. The Verdict

The judge lifted himself out of his chair with both palms flat on the
    table.
"Susanna," he said, in a low voice.
Susanna looked at the people for the first time during her trial,
gradually casting her gaze about the circle,

staring directly into the faces of the armed good citizens of her
     country.
Her dark complexion was the night sky,
her eyes, star sapphires.
The citizens in the circle around her looked up and down and to the
     side,
everywhere but at her,
their hands fidgeting awkwardly with their weapons.
Susanna's eyes, completing the circle, met the judge's,
and he spoke again.
"Do you have anything to say for yourself, Susanna?"
Susanna shook her head once back and forth.
"In that case I sentence you to death."

The two elders stood, holding on to each other for support,
gaping one last time at the sentenced woman.
Then they melted into the crowd.
Four guards who had been flanking the judge stepped forward.
Two of them removed the table and chairs,
while the other two grabbed Susanna's arms.
They led her to the center of the circle.
The sun was directly over Susanna's head now.
She stared down into the tiny oval shadow between her feet.
The armed good citizens marched forward,
closing in on her,
each gripping a weapon brought from home.
One of the guards released Susanna's arm.
He grabbed her cloth belt and began to untie the knot,
for it was the custom in this country to execute a guilty woman
     naked,

to bring final shame to her, her memory and her family.
Some of the good citizens in the circle surrounding Susanna
were already shaking their bars,
their shards of glass
their shears
their hammers and their guns
with heightened anticipation for the end.
It was then that Susanna spoke her mind,
her words pointed,
echoing loudly inside the circle.

"You must not do this!
How can you look indifferently upon a naked woman when you
        condemn such nakedness in her?
The evidence presented against me is false.
I have betrayed no one, let alone myself.
If you kill me here my death will enter into the conscience of each
        and every one of you.
You will never rid yourselves of its memory until your dying day.
Do not let this crime occur today
for your own sake
if not for mine!"

The judge, blotting the sweat on his brow with the back of his hand,
        admonished the guards.
"What is holding you up? Get on with it, will you?
We don't have all the time in the world."
"Kill her the way she is!" shouted a man in the crowd,
though no one knew which man he was.
"Why wait? We have lives to get on with!" screamed a woman in the

crowd,
though no one knew which woman she was.
The armed good citizens were anxious to have Susanna off their
        mind,
dead and buried
over and done with.
The second guard flashed a thin-lipped smile, nodding around the
        circle.
"I have done it. I have undone the knot," he boasted.
"This knot was nothing, nothing at all."
He began to unravel the belt that held Susanna's dark-blue robe
        together.
And as he did, the armed good citizens took another step forward
then another and another
forming a gigantic eye,
with Susanna the iris.
She was no more than a small black dot
in a sun about to explode.

Her robe was now untied, half open, hanging loose on her.
Each guard was gripping a shoulder, looking to the judge for the
        nod.
At his nod, the robe would be yanked off Susanna's body,
the guards would recede,
and her flesh would be cut and snipped, clubbed, pierced and sliced
from her bones
by her people.

The chain of clouds had sunk below the horizon.
No shade existed in that world.

And yet, despite the glaring abundance of light,
there seemed no space for truth to slip, unseen, into sight.

Just then, however, a young man's voice was heard coming from the
        crowd.
"Wait. Do not go ahead with this!"
The man now appeared, as if from nowhere, beside Susanna.
With a head of straggly dark hair and a black face covered with
        pimples, he could not have been a day over sixteen.
"I for one will not have the death of this woman on my conscience.
I will not allow my conscience to be dictated to by the phrases of
        hypocritical authority!"
Was it the innocent sincerity of the young man's voice?
Or was it the earnestness and passion that he radiated?
Be whatever, the citizens found their eyes turning once again to the
        judge.
They were curious to see
whether he would give the nod for the execution to commence,
or whether he would allow the young black man a say.

"What are you on about, young man? Speak up," bellowed the judge.
And, for the moment, all weapons were lowered.
All eyes rested on the young man.
Picking up the cloth belt and handing it to Susanna,
he bowed deeply to the judge,
then bowed just as deeply to the citizens who formed the eye.

This is what he said:

3. The Defense

"My name is Daniel. I have never spoken to this woman,
though I have been in her garden.
(Immediately the thought entered a hundred heads: Could this be the
    man who committed the sinful act with Susanna?)
I received permission from her housekeeper to tend the garden.
Though uneducated, I have much rapport with plants and know them
    well.
The garden in this woman's house is a particularly wonderful one.
There are apricot and fig and olive trees there, and date palms too.
There are lovely lilies and hyacinths, and there is myrtle and boxwood.
There is hibiscus and hollyhock, whose flowers predict the rain,
and hyssop and dill, and dandelion.
My people say dandelion resembles my character, though I see no
    resemblance myself.
Around the pond grow poppies, violets and thistles, and a weeping
    willow hangs well over it. In addition, there are …"
"Young man!" intervened the judge, brusquely.
"This is not a lecture theater of botany, nor is it the stage for a flower
    show.
A woman's life is at stake!"
Daniel cleared his throat and, with a modest bow to the judge,
    continued.

"Excuse me, sir, I do get carried away when discussing plant life.
But there is a point to which I am getting, if by beating around a bush.
(The judge chuckled at this, for he was a judge who appreciated the
    unexpected turn of wit.)

You see, sir, and fine citizens of our country,
a woman who would so vigorously protest over the violation of
        modesty must be virtuous.
Such a woman cares about herself and her people.
She would not betray them.
I ask that the two elders, her prosecutors, come forward, if they
        themselves have nothing to hide.
(The two elders reappeared shoulder to shoulder in the center of the
        eyelike circle.)
Thank you, gentlemen. I hope that your integrity carries the same
        weight of authority that you claim from this community."
At this, Daniel approached the judge and whispered into his ear.
The judge, pursing his ample lips, nodded his head twice.
Daniel returned to the center of the eye and continued,
now in a more gentle voice than before.

"The judge has given me permission to ask a single question of each
        elder.
Will the first elder please step forward. Thank you."
After a moment in discussion with the first elder, Daniel summoned
        the second elder and asked him a single question as well.
Satisfied, he once again took his place beside Susanna.
Their shadows merged into one behind them.

"Thank you, judge. Thank you, elders. Thank you, fine citizens.
I have something to report to you all.
This woman is innocent!"
(A sigh rushed through the circle … was this a sigh of relief or of
        disbelief? It was impossible to tell.)
"How can you be sure?" asked the judge.

"I am sure," replied Daniel.

"You see, I put one simple question, separately, to each eye witness.

That question was:

What plant were you hiding behind when this woman allegedly
     committed her sin?

The first elder, who had accused her of being enticing by merely
     disrobing, answered, 'A giant broom tree.'

Well, my good friends, there is indeed a giant broom tree in the
     garden.

I have tended it myself, marveling at its exquisite yellow flowers.

But I say to you now, we can sweep this man's false testimony away!

For one thing, the giant broom is located in the far corner of the
     garden,

out of earshot of the pond,

particularly when that ear belongs to such an elderly elder as our
     first eye witness.

He could not possibly have heard the words that this woman spoke
     to her maids.

But kindly continue to lend me your ears, my fellow citizens,

for there is further damning evidence to nullify the groundless
     accusations

we have all heard in this square today.

I put the very same question to the second elder:

Behind what plant were you and your friend hiding when you
     observed the accused go through unspeakable acts with an
     unidentifiable man.

And he replied, 'Why, uh … the leafy rue bush.'

Ah now, there is indeed a leafy rue bush in the garden of this
     woman's home,

a bush whose leaves are bitter,

becoming, much like our two prosecutors, ever more bitter
as they dry out with time.
(Once again the judge chuckled, this time more heartily than before,
    until his chuckle turned into a cough and he begged one of his
    guards to slap him on the back to arrest it.)
So you see, one and all,
as a consequence,
this second elder, standing shamelessly before you,
will now rue the day that he accused this honest woman of adultery.
For it was these two men,
dried out
bitter
and withered in pompous old age,
drunk on the spirits of self-importance,
driven by a hideous and repulsive lust …
it was they who planned to defile her!
They attacked her by that pond.
And when she refused to give in to them,
fighting back and resisting,
they concocted their plot to do her in.
Theirs is the crime, my friends.
If you have a mind to punish someone, punish *them*."

Daniel, exhausted and bathed in sweat,
wiped his pimply face with his sleeve and joined the circle.
The judge glared at the two elders.
Their necks were bent, like old trees,
and they stared into the roots of the Earth,
seeing nothing.
The armed good citizens,

their weapons poised once again,
turned their gaze on them.
They would have cut and snipped, clubbed, pierced and sliced their
　　　flesh at the drop of a hat.
But the judge pointed his knuckled finger straight up to the top of
　　　the sky and said …
"Leave them be. I will deal with them myself."
(At this the elders got down on their hands and knees and bowed to
　　　the judge, their foreheads touching the searing ground.)

The citizens began to disperse,
taking their weapons home with them,
as Susanna, tying her cloth belt tightly around her waist,
wove her way among them.
They made a path for her, lowering their eyes
as she passed them by.

When she arrived home
her husband was waiting for her.
He hadn't known what to think till then.

Susanna walked by him,
went to her room
and shut the door.

JOB

1. The Marketplace

Sunday in the city, an ant colony of life ...
lines of scrawny men bent under their weight in goods,
bags and bales and crates converging on the square,
piles of almonds, cliffs of cabbage, mountains of dates,
figs and olives and oils and myriad foods,
men building stalls or taking them down,
tents boasting jugglers and prophets and clowns,
soldiers on horseback, clanking their armor,
rulers and ruled, merchant and farmer,
cartloads of slaves moaning in pain,
beggars caught in invisible chains.
They were all there, the rich and the poor and the few in between,
the din of the city, a barricade of music,
its notes spiraling up, like the thinnest columns of smoke,
into the clouds, the clouds bulging with the uproar,
turning from ominous grey to tar.
Large hot drops began to fall on the marketplace,
and the din of city was superceded by the babble of a storm.
The colony scattered.
The rulers and the ruled fled under roofs.
The prophets and the clowns retreated to their tents.
Even the beggars took refuge under generously spreading trees.
All talk of commerce ceased.

All gossip trailed off.
The heavens opened.

And yet a single man remained unchanged and unmoved.
He was sitting beside the city wall that could not protect him.
The dust around him became a black torrent of mud like the tar sky
        itself.
His name was Job and he was oblivious to this onslaught.
Nothing could get to him.
Nothing could touch him.
Strings of hair, braided with dirt, tumbled over his forehead,
        patching his eyes.
No matter … an eye is no longer needed, he reckoned.
Nothing mattered to Job.
"Let the mud pouring into my eyes blind me,
let the clamor enveloping my ears deafen me,
let the water falling from the sky drown me," he thought.
He regarded the marketplace through bars of hair,
cupped an ear in his palm
and licked his parted lips with a cracked tongue.
He suddenly felt the hairs on his body stand on end
then watched, detached,
as lightning struck a discarded buckle near his feet.
(Who put it there?)
The buckle flared, and Job's body was thrown against the wall.
Just as the back of his head slammed against brick,
a clap of thunder rattled his brain,
so loudly that his ear drums shuddered.
A ringing in his head carried with it a rude voice, telling him …
"Job, you are nothing.

Job, you are worthless.
Were you to die here and now,
even the condemned slaves would point their death finger at you,
even the wretched beggars would mock you in contemptuous
    gesture,
even the scavenging dogs would avoid your carcass like the plague.
Job, you are nothing, nothing, nothing.
Nothing in life and nothing in death.
YOU
are
nothing!"

Rain battered Job's head, chest, arms and legs like dulled nails.
He shook violently from the cold.
Every patch of his body felt a different kind of pain
stinging
pounding
dulling
penetrating.
His bowels wrenched into a thick length of dried twine,
as he sat still in the mud of his own excrement.
Another clap of thunder, another ringing in his head …
"Take yourself in, Job, look at you.
Your back is to the wall.
Your body is bathed in the filth of your own making.
You deserve this, Job!
You deserve this because of the man you are!"

Job looked around, the sole witness in the sweep of the market.
"Deserted," he thought.

"The rain has let up, and yet there is not a soul in sight.
Ah, the entire world has ceased to exist.
I am the only person left now.
I must represent all people."

Just then a single figure appeared from behind one of the tents.
It was the figure of a little girl, no more than ten or eleven years old.
She was dressed in a dress of light-yellow linen,
a shawl of bright red hibiscus flowers around her head,
a striped cloth bag on her arm and sandals tied at the ankles.
Honey-colored locks of hair peeked out from the shawl,
resting lightly on her shoulders.
She crossed the marketplace square and walked directly toward Job.
Seeing her, he pressed himself against the wall.
The little girl stopped in front of him and, bending over, asked …
"Why didn't you shelter yourself from the rain?"
Job stared at her without answering.
"Are you in pain?
Where does it hurt?"

Job wanted to tell her of the arthritis that was slicing his every joint,
of the wheezing in his every nighttime breath,
of the vomiting that overcame him with every meager meal,
of the hernia that wrung his loins with every step,
of the headaches that stabbed his brain every morning,
of the sores on his body that burst and flowed with horrid pus,
of his gums that bled like tiny fountains,
of his scalp that burned as if scorched by the sun,
and his toes that itched so much that he had scratched away the skin
    between them.

But what would a little girl know about all that?
So he just continued to stare fixedly at her
with the whites of his eyes as yellow as the fabric of her dress,
        wondering …
"Why isn't she repelled by my looks and my stink?"
The little girl stretched out her hand to brush the hair from Job's
        eyes.
He recoiled like a cornered snake.
She removed her shawl to cover his shivering knees,
and he drew them in, locking his arms around them.
She took a small polished gourd from her cloth bag,
uncorked it and put it to his ulcerated lips.
He clamped them shut like a vice.
"Can no one help you?" she asked.
"No," answered Job in a whisper. "No one can help me."
The little girl corked her gourd and put it back in her bag.
She stood, wiped her hand on her dress and covered her head with
        her shawl.
Shafts of sunlight fell onto the marketplace like curtain drops,
turning droplets in the air into slivers of light.
And, as the glass curtain drew up into the sky,
the colony returned, to its very same places …
soldiers and slaves
merchants and farmers
prophets and clowns.
Even the beggars had a place set aside for them.
It was as if there had been no interruption to their lives.
They resumed their stances, triumphant and cowering,
posed their poses, demanding and obsequious,
reiterated their words, harsh and fantastic.

And yet, during the brief, already forgotten downpour,
Job had relived half a lifetime of anguish.

The little girl turned her back on him,
retracing her steps across the square.
"Wait!" cried Job, shading his eyes from the blinding light.
"Please! Wait …."
The girl swiveled around.
Her locks lifted off her shoulders.
"Come back," cried Job.
"Please come back here.
I want to tell you. I want to tell you something."

2. "My Life"

This is what Job told the girl by the wall on the edge of the
        marketplace square:

I used to lay in my bed in my home in my village,
my wife and little children soundly asleep under my roof,
        thinking …
"Why did this happen to me?
Why in my village?
Why under my roof?
Why in my bed?
There are countless villages, roofs, beds, people in the world,
and they have not encountered the marvels of fate that I have."
You see, I had been supremely blessed.
It was not due to my kindliness that my wife was devoted and

      capable.
Nor was it due to my judiciousness that my children were good.
People who knew me, and many who didn't, praised my actions.
I was called a good man,
a righteous provider for all in my circle and many outside it.
I was given awards for virtuous nature,
trophies for charitable deeds.
My drawers brimmed with fancily written plaudits.
My mantelpiece was cluttered with the prizes of acclaim.
Yet, why were these accolades bestowed upon me?
Not because of the man I was.
I did not deceive myself in this.
Whatever was me came from the whims of fortune.
Another man in a village that is not mine
under a roof not mine
in a bed not my own
could have been given possession of such riches.
It was all due to an accident of time and place
in favor of a man named Job.
Why was such good fortune bestowed on *me*?

Then I was thrown into chaos.
My mind could scarcely focus on one tragedy than did a second one
      befall me
and a third … a fourth … a fifth.
One after the other, the skin of blessings peeled away,
the fortune dwindled, all benefit gone, up in smoke.
My children were crushed and killed by the giant hand of a cyclone.
My cows, donkeys and camels were stolen by enemies.
My sheep were destroyed by lightning fire.

My own body fell to pieces, assaulted by disease and rot.
Yet, as the disorder of thought and frantic pleading gave way to calm,
I came to accept my inflictions.
I knew that I deserved them no more or less than I deserved their
        absence,
that every single joy, trivial or mighty, contained its curse,
and the wonderment felt for my miraculous good fortune
was no different from that now felt for my grotesque ill luck.

Accusations flew into my face, like pellets flung from a thousand fists.
Job the child abuser.
Job the adulterer.
Job the liar.
Job the thief.
Job the man whose inhumanity will condemn him to an eternity of
        grief.
The parchment of accolades withered.
The trophies on the mantelpiece shattered and crumbled.
My friends deserted me, accusing me of disloyalty and corruption.
My wife rebuked me and, revolted by my demeanor,
walked out of the house and into the bed of another man.

And I asked myself …
"Which Job is the true one?
Am I not like this?
Is this not my natural state?"
And I told myself …
"I accept what I am today.
Why not me? WHY NOT ME?"

Throughout the fall into my abyss,
I peered through the blackness.
I saw other men and women, some above me, some below,
some rising, some falling,
and I knew that they were there by the same graces that I was,
the graces of arbitrary design,
of nature's wicked sidelong glance that catches you,
you and no one else,
seizes you and hurls you upward or downward.
"This is what happens to *you*?"

As Job told the little girl the story of his life
and how he came to be so degraded,
bystanders passed near them and spat on him.
Children took balls of fresh mud in their fists and heaved them at
        his groin.
Priests looked down on him with much too much pity,
and well-dressed women hurried by, covering the cheek that faced
        him.
As for Job,
he wiped away neither the spit nor the mud,
nor did he cringe under the gazes of pity and shock.
He was the man sitting by the wall on the edge of the marketplace
        square,
and if not him, then some other would be in his place,
as chance would have it.
"The wraith's fate," he thought, "is temporarily mine."
And he accepted it for what it was.

Job smiled up to the girl, who had not taken her eyes off of him.

Neither had noticed that a half-ring of people had formed around
        them.
Jeering voices mingled into a war cry of abuse,
and the coarse sound struck the wall,
echoing back throughout the square.
The echo became louder and louder, as if amplified by the ceiling of
        the sky,
and the louder the people shouted, grimacing in anger and pain,
the greater was the echo of their own voices in their ears.
"Get away from Job!
Job is base!
Job is odious!
Job has been condemned!
Job is doomed! Doomed! Doomed!! Doomed!!!
No one in the world is as putrid and deserving of death as Job!
Die now, Job.
Yes. Die for us now!"
But the people were soon forced to scatter, covering their ears.
They were repelled by the echo of their own words.

Shortly after nightfall, Job and the little girl beside him were joined
        by another figure.
Job's wife had come for him.
She sat next to him and took his hand in hers.
"I'm sorry," she said, putting his palm to her lips.
"Don't do that," said Job. "My hands are filthier than filth."
"Then that filth will be mine as well," she said.
She helped him up,
and the three of them, with the little girl in the middle,
walked through the marketplace, hand in hand.

The good people of the city, of whatever rank and station …
merchant and farmer, prophet and clown,
soldier, slave and beggar, the ruler and their ruled …
stood in absolute silence,
gawking at them as if they were animals suddenly transformed
into human beings.
Job smiled generously to all of them, whoever they were:
today's friend and foe, one and the same,
tomorrow's acquaintance and stranger, with or without name.
And Job, the same man that he always was,
irrespective of fortune's impulse,
recalled the questions that he had asked himself what seemed to him
      an age ago.
"Why did this happen to me?
Why in my village?
Why under my roof?
Why in my bed?
There are countless villages, roofs, beds, people in this world,
and they have not encountered the marvels of fate that I have."

I am them, blessed and unblessed
in one.

3. The Same Man As Always

After that, Job's wife gave birth to several children.
Job worked hard, possessed many animals and regained his stature,
though he was still troubled by
arthritis, asthma, indigestion, rash, bleeding gums, headache, reflux

       and a newly acquired gout in his big left toe,
among other things.
If this was more than one's fair share of affliction,
he never questioned it.

And every day without fail,
just before sunset,
whatever the weather, rain or shine,
he returned to the wall and sat in the same old place,
in his old rags,
by the edge of the marketplace square.
And all the people who passed him by,
whatever their rank or station,
nodded and bowed, nodded and bowed,
full of the highest praises for the man
on whom fortune has so generously smiled.
After all, they reckoned, it couldn't have happened to a nicer man
than Job.

And Job always smiled back,
to every single one of them,
for he was the same man
as he always was.

JONAH

1. Dead to the Entire World

It seemed to come out of the blue,
a storm that turned the rolling plains of the sea to mountains,
their summits, snow capped,
their crests frothing,
scattering into the air like scallions, settling on slopes
before sliding down on an avalanche of water.

On the tip of just one of those soaring waves sat a modest ship,
its crew clinging for dear life to mast and rail,
staring down the slide into a swirling hole that they took for hell.
Meanwhile, the ship pitched and rocked, pitched and rocked,
standing out of the water like a terrified shrieking animal.
The men shouted desperately to each other,
but their words were shredded by the gale,
and all that could be heard were splinters of sound.
"Wh ..."
"Aa ..."
"H-rrr ..."
"Gggggggggg ..."
With each flash of lightning, men gazed at each other under the
        flapping wings of sail,
a red terror in their eyes,
mouths agape with white-hot teeth,

each one thinking the very same thing while gripping his fistful of
     wood …
"Save me!
Save me!
Save ME!"

When they peered once again into the swirling hole of the sea,
standing, crouching, kneeling just below the ceiling of the sky,
a tail of lightning lit up the world under their feet,
allowing them an instant to see down the long blackened tube.
An unholy "CREAK!" was heard,
and the men hugged their little round of dead wood more tightly,
convinced that the ship would soon split in two,
closing around them like a traveling bag,
packing them, locked inside, down the spout of the sea.
While the ship rested for a moment on the plateau of a crest,
its crew now moved about the deck,
madly hurling cargo overboard.
The captain went to one of his men, and shouted in his ear.
"We seemed to have lost a hand!"
The man looked around the deck.
"No. He's down in the hold."
"What's he doing there?" asked the captain, wiping a sheet of salty
     water from his face.
"Last thing I knew he was sleeping."
"Sleeping?"
"Yeah. That's right. Dead to the world."
"Dead to the world, is he?"
"In a manner of speaking."
"We'll see to that!" hollered the captain straight up to the top of the
     sky.

And frowning like the devil,
with the corners of his mouth seeming to reach beyond his ears,
he grabbed an amphora of olive oil in both hands,
held it high above his head as a priest does an animal about to be
        sacrificed,
and tossed it far over the side of the ship, screaming once again to
        the high heavens.
"We shall see to THAT!"
When the amphora struck the slant of the wave,
it started to roll down it,
leaving a thin trail of light-green oil in its wake,
a gleaming line leading farther and farther down,
sticking to the glassy water's surface long after the amphora was
        devoured
by what the men took for the mouth of hell.

When the captain reached the hold, sure enough,
the unaccounted for hand was fast asleep,
his palms together, a pillow for his cheek,
and a closed smile on his pleasant lips.
Indeed, he was by the standards of any time, place or circumstance,
dead to the entire world.
The captain grasped his shoulders and shook him like a cloth doll.
The man opened his eyes,
and now parting his lips in an even more innocent smile than
        before, said …
"Oh."
He had been so soundly asleep that he did not recognize the captain.
"You're Jonah, aren't you!" yelled the captain in a voice so gruff that
        it nearly knocked Jonah out of his hanging net bed.

For a moment even Jonah wasn't sure that he was Jonah,
and, clinging to the captain's coat, he said …
"Jonah? Yes. I am!"
The captain stood Jonah on his two feet and dragged him to the deck.
The rest of the crew, frantically throwing the last of the cargo into the
    sea, were fit to be tied.
"If we don't get out of this, it'll be Jonah's fault," cried one hand,
losing his balance and dropping a sealed jug of date wine on his toes.
"Jonah could've been helping us, but instead he ran down to hide."
"Ouch!" cried another hand, cracked on the head by a loose piece of
    rigging.
"Our ship will be lighter without Jonah," yelled a third hand.
He lunged toward the still half-dazed Jonah, lost his footing
and landed smack on his bony behind.
Jonah was now surrounded by a circle of hands,
their coin-like sunken stares piercing him,
their outstretched fingers, shards of glass about to slice his flesh into a
    hundred bits.

Once again the heavens rumbled,
and the white caps of the waves were brushed into the chaos of the
    sky.
Jonah, alone in the middle of the ship, finally came to his senses and
    said to all of the men …
"It is my fault that you are in such mortal danger.
I shouldn't even be on this ship by all rights.
I am running away.
I did not want to witness the destruction of a city.
So I went the other way.
This ship happened to be going that way.

It is only by accident that I am among you.
You may call me a coward, if you wish."
And at that, the rest of the crew, again holding fast to mast and rail,
        shouted in a mocking tone.
"Coward!
Coward!
Coward!
The life of men like Jonah isn't worth a rodent's breath.
It's rats like Jonah who deserve to die a painful death!"
And, even though Jonah knew that the men were talking about him,
he had to admit that they probably had a point.
Ever since he was a child he had been running away from fights.
Even a petty argument with his elder brother about who lost their
        father's fishhook left him cowering in tears,
and that was even before the argument started.
Jonah knew there was only one thing to do.
So, stepping carefully across the slick of the deck,
he made his way to the prow.
He hopped onto the rail and turned to face the deck.
Teetering and reeling,
he waved his arms for balance, and called to all the hands.
"You will all be better off without Jonah."
All the hands nodded in agreement, applauding him.
Jonah applauded back to them, for he did not doubt their bravery.
But this caused him to lose his footing on the slippery rail.
At that moment Jonah believed,
deep in his heart of hearts,
that the world was no place for a man like him.

Jonah fell backward, listing toward a massive wall of water.
His body flipped, grazing that unforgiving wall.
As he descended fathom by fathom,
disappearing into the swirling black of the hole,
the gale became a wind and the wind a mild breeze.
Soon the waves were an indistinguishable part of a plate-like sea.
The men on the ship, twisting their neck here and there,
could now take in the entire sweep of the horizon.
The sun shone and the sky turned blue.
The men embraced each other and jumped for joy,
some gliding over the deck in a dance of life.
"The worst is over, men," said the captain,
spitting out a string of seaweed that had lodged between his teeth.
"Thank your lucky stars."
It wasn't long before they were ready to sail again on a calmed sea,
each man devising his own side of the story to tell all who would
        listen.
In not one of those stories, however,
no matter how different in detail and purport they were,
was there so much as a mention of Jonah.
As far as the men on the ship were concerned,
Jonah was forgotten
and as good as dead.

2. The Giant Fish

To tell the truth, Jonah *was* as good as dead.
But that didn't actually make him dead.
You would have thought that people finding themselves cast into the
        sea like unwanted bait would balk at their fate.

But Jonah not only accepted his fate,
he seemed to relish its trials.
He thought to himself, while plunging down the tube of the sea …
"At least I won't have to fight with anybody down here."

As he was falling, a certain peace settled around him.
He looked past his feet.
But no matter how he strained and squinted his eyes,
he could not see to the bottom of the cone of water.
Just when he was wiggling his toes, which were itchy from the air
         streaming up at them,
a giant fish broke through the wall of the tube above him.
With its tail still inside the water,
it opened its mouth wide enough to accommodate a ship of modest
         size,
and readily swallowed Jonah whole,
before shooting into the opposite wall of the cone.
The cone swirled and spiraled shut,
and Jonah, immersed in a warmish liquid,
wondered to himself …
"Why has the light suddenly disappeared?"

Jonah had been, in one bright moment, swallowed up.
Before he knew it, Jonah found himself standing up to his ears in
         water,
or, at least, in a liquid that resembled water.
He brought his sticky hand through the liquid up to his nose.
"Vinegar! I love vinegar!" he thought, licking his lips of the stuff.
A school of a thousand phosphorescent squid streamed before his
         eyes,

followed by a score of sleek porpoises, rolling as they swam,
and on their tail a killer whale.
Jonah ducked under the thick liquid, holding his breath,
crouching on the floor of the giant fish's belly.
He craned his neck, catching sight of the killer whale sailing above
     him.
In the light created by the phosphorescent squid,
the porpoises and the killer whale
were being whooshed about in all directions,
agitated and churned,
until their bodies were finally ripped to strips and shreds,
then sucked into a snake-like chute at the belly's end.
Jonah treaded the sticky liquid as diligently as he could,
lest he, too, be carried along to that end.
And as he treaded, the level of the liquid gradually dropped,
from his chin to his navel
from his navel to his knee
from his knee to his ankle
until he found himself standing in a warm shallow phosphorescent
     pool.
With eyes like saucers, he stared around the slimy cavern,
fully realizing where he was for the first time,
and hoping that the crew of the ship were as safe as he.

3. The Sunlit Beach

Jonah spent three days and three nights inside the giant fish,
most of the time with his two feet planted on its belly's floor.
At those times he could even walk around a bit,

feeling his way along the sloshy walls.
When the level of the sticky vinegary liquid rose, Jonah rose with it,
treading with all his might.
It was on these occasions that enormous schools of fish of every
        variety streamed by,
and Jonah was able to thrust his hand out and catch some.
He feasted on shrimp and mullet
that came down the gullet
and cod and bass
that floated past.
He ate all the flake
he could possibly take
and even ate ray
that happened his way.
All in all, Jonah ate up his fill,
drawing the line at sea slugs, urchins … and krill.
Jonah knew he was moving, too, but only because of the changing
        light.
"This fish must be swimming close to the surface of the sea now," he
        thought to himself.
Light filtered through the skin,
and through its grey cast
he could make out the smooth belly's inner walls.
He thought to himself, smiling his innocent smile …
"I've never lived in such spacious surroundings as these before."

Jonah wouldn't have found himself in that giant fish's belly if it
        hadn't been for his father.
His father had wanted him to go to a city that was about to be
        destroyed.

"If you see the miracles that our people can accomplish when they
        wreak havoc on our enemies," his father had told him,
"you, too, will become strong."
"But Father," Jonah had said,
"I don't want to be strong if that is what I have to do to be strong.
All I want to be is a fisherman and go through life without seeing
        men kill other men."
"Such a life is impossible," said his father angrily.
"You are too young to understand the nature of our world.
Now, go tonight to the harbor and get on the ship.
Get yourself to the city that is about to be destroyed.
Feast your eyes on the feats of our soldiers.
When you come back, you will be a man."

Jonah did go to the harbor that night like his father told him.
But, at the last moment, he boarded a ship going in the opposite
        direction.
That was the ship caught up in the storm.
That was the storm that angered the crew.
That was the crew that prodded him into the sea.
That was the sea that harbored the fish.
And that was the fish that swallowed him up.
And just as those memories entered and left his head,
Jonah was thrown clean off his feet,
shaken and stirred in the cauldron of the giant fish's belly,
until he did not know which end was up and which side which.
The grey inside the belly turned paler and paler,
as Jonah was propelled once again feet first at breakneck speed,
wrapped in a dense tangle of seaweed.
The seaweed clenched his throat, twisting like octopus tentacles,

and Jonah was unable to breathe.
He tried to grab the seaweed and pull it away,
but he lacked the strength.
The last thing that he saw before passing out was beads of bright
    yellow light between his toes.
The giant fish vomited Jonah up its gullet and onto a sandbar by a
    beach.
A gentle tide lifted him up onto the shore.
When Jonah came to he was on his back.
Seaweed was wrapped around his entire body, like swaddling clothes
    on a baby,
but there was none around his neck.
A crab was perched on top of his head,
its body and pincers forming a crown.
The crab had survived by clinging to Jonah's scalp.
Jonah looked around.
He had no idea where he was.
Two children, a boy and a girl, came running up,
and they spoke to him.
But he couldn't understand a word they were saying.

"I would rather spend the rest of my days in a fish's belly," he said to
    them, sitting up,
"than be a man in a land where the strong rule wickedly over the
    weak and proclaim themselves 'good.'"

The children giggled and ran away.
After all, a strange man in a seaweed suit
with a crab clinging to his scalp
is an unusual sight.

Jonah got up on his feet,
wriggled the seaweed down to the sand,
and, holding the crab proudly in both hands in front of him,
walked along the sunlit beach,
beaming.

THE GOOD SAMARITAN

1. The Road

When on the road you can leave your shame behind.
Or so goes the old proverb.

There is no telling what can happen when you are on a road.
Some people feel liberated, elated to leave their home.
They encounter places and sounds and smells and other people
they never imagined existed before.
They find new people to be friends with.
They discover new lovers to be happy with.
And sometimes they even settle down for good
in a place where a road has led them.
But there are other kinds of occurrences that a road witnesses as
       well.
A road captures all that takes place on or beside it.
It takes in the good with the bad.
A road is the old proverb's silent witness:
When on the road you can leave your shame behind.

Now, the road in this story is, in a word, indistinguishable from
       thousands of other roads like it.
It wound from place to place like the next road.
It straightened out at times, stretching into an unfamiliar distance,
its twin rows of poplars dwindling and vanishing below the horizon.

The road ran smooth and rough, depending on the weather.
And it had your standard number of potholes.
It was dusty in dry weather,
and muddy in wet.
Its shoulders boasted both impressive boulders and commonplace
      gravel,
depending on the lie of the land.
Some of its scenery was utterly spectacular,
with meadows of flowers heading for the hills,
and farms and vineyards and orchards as far as a traveler's eye could
      see.
But some of the landscape was barren, drab and stark,
especially where the road cut through lands
that had known drought or flood … or, worst of all, war.
In short, this road ran the gamut of sights.
There was nothing under the sun that it hadn't seen.

The people who lived near the road rarely gave this a second
      thought.
To them the road was just a span of earth to cross fields on
to carry fruit on
to go to market on
to visit relatives on.
It didn't even have a name.
It was just "the road."
"Take the road," people would say to each other.
And everybody knew exactly which road they were talking about.
When something happened to a traveler on the road,
by fortune or misfortune,
they paid scant attention to it.

"After all, it's the road's problem,
not ours," they all said.
"Let the people down the road deal with it.
That's where the traveler was coming from."
"Let the people up the road handle it.
That's where the traveler was destined."

And so, years and decades and centuries passed uneventfully
for the people who lived by the side of the road.
Look up from the road on bright days long long ago in its past
and what can you see in the blare of the sun?
The thick soles of soldiers' boots, marching in rhythm
(this always caused the most damage).
Heels of thin cloth, barely denting the soft soil,
and bare feet, too, of all sizes, some with scars or half-open cuts,
others with skin wrinkled and hardened with time,
trampling through the dirt
oblivious to hurt
trudging over clay
day by day by day by day.
The wheels of wagons churned up the road,
scattering fine powder to the wind.
Carts made grooves in the road,
hurtling pointed rocks into the weeds.
Paws and hoofs and beaks pierced its surface,
leaving their little mark for the time being.
Blood too spilled onto the road, eventually seeping into it.
And though, before long, the blood would disappear from the
        surface,
it would become a part of the road,

no less than the earth itself.

The people who lived by the side of the road
failed to notice the most unimaginable things that happened on it.
Farmers tended their fields with their backs to the road.
Fruitpickers buried their heads in the leaves of their trees.
Shepherds never took eyes off their flocks.
Children were beaten
Women were raped
Men were murdered
on the road as it passed by their homes.
"We cannot stop these things from happening," the people said,
wherever they lived along the road.
"It's the road's fault.
It wouldn't happen here if it weren't for that road.
Those people are not from here. They are from somewhere else."
Some people wanted to live where there was no road
so that they wouldn't have to ignore what happened on it.

One day, under a brilliant blue sky, a child was taken onto the road.
The boy, only eleven years old, a farmer's youngest son,
was grabbed by passing soldiers.
Four soldiers held the little boy,
each gripping an arm or a leg,
and flung him into their cart like a rag.
The father, a farmer of flax, came running through his fields.
But by the time he reached the road he was too late.
He barely caught sight of the cart disappearing
between the fading poplar trees.
The father collapsed on the road and wept uncontrollably.

His tears, too, seeped deep into the road.
No one was there who could help him.
No one was there to comfort him.
Just a single man on a road, long ago in the past, seen by no one.

That sort of thing happened, too, on our road
in the place where, people say, shame had been left behind.

2. The Man Who Was Robbed

Many decades after the kidnapping of the child by the soldiers
and the father's uncontrollable weeping,
a man found his way to the very same spot on the road.
It just so happens that an elm tree had grown by the side of the road
        there,
though no one knew how it got there in the first place.
There were no elms in that region to give seed.

Now, no one knows what kind of a man this was or why he was on
        the road.
It isn't recorded.
The only people who saw him coming were wayward bandits,
and they were never caught.
This man had stopped to rest under the elm tree.
The day had been brutally hot, and it was shady under there.
He rested, leaning his back against the trunk, and drank from his
        flask.
And just as he was wiping his mouth with the back of his hand,
he closed his eyes tightly, drew in a deep breath, and smiled.

He didn't know what hit him.

It was no doubt a heavy stick or club.

With his head reeling, he looked up.

In the blur of his eyes he saw branches pitching and swirling, as if in a
powerful wind.

Then he felt another blow to his head and all went as black as night.

How long after was it that the first traveler appeared?

To judge by the angle of the shadow cast by the elm tree

it was approaching late afternoon.

The traveler was a priest, a most devout and pious man,

known for his profound knowledge of moral doctrine.

Dressed in a robe of brightly colored linen,

with shoes of pigskin on his feet,

and deep furrows in his brow,

he was on his way to meet his distant worshippers.

He plodded along the road with the weight of the world on his
conscience.

Catching sight of the elm tree from afar,

he decided to rest his weary bones under it.

But as he neared the elm, he was stopped dead in his tracks.

For under it was the man who had been robbed, not moving a muscle.

The man had been stripped of everything on his person.

He was totally naked, his cuts and bruises exposed for all the world to
see.

He had been mutilated around the pelvis and beaten about the head.

Suddenly the man stirred, lifting an arm onto his chest.

The priest, now furrowing his brow even more deeply, thought …

"Who is this man under the elm tree?

Is he a good man or a bad one?

Is he a rich man or a poor one?"
The priest could not tell.
All he knew was that the man was helpless and in pain.
This sight stirred the priest to the quick,
and, feeling a burst of fresh energy,
he hurried up to the spot where the elm tree was
and swiftly passed it by with jaunty steps,
skirting along the opposite edge of the road.
"The Incident Under the Elm Tree," as he came to call it, gave the
      priest new strength and stronger faith.
He could not wait to join his worshippers and tell them of the awful
      things
that are occurring on "our very own roads."

How long after was it that the second traveler appeared?
To judge by the depth of the shadows
it was nearing the moments of twilight.
This traveler was an upstanding citizen of his community,
known for staunch successes in the world of commerce.
Dressed in a smoothly ironed grey suit of clothes,
with shoes of cowhide on his feet,
he ambled along the road with the burden of influence on his
      conscience.
Catching sight of the elm tree from afar,
he decided to rest his weary bones under it.
But as he approached the elm, he was stopped dead in his tracks.
The man who was robbed was in a sitting position, not moving a
      muscle.
He was still naked, with blood congealed about his pelvis and head.
"Who could this man be?" thought the pillar of commerce.

"He could not be a man of influence, for I do not recognize him."
The sight of the man, helpless and in pain, did not move this
          important man.
He simply walked past him, skirting the opposite edge of the road,
shaking his head in dismay at the state of the world,
and hurrying forward to tend to vital affairs.

The shadow of the elm tree lengthened,
its outlines gradually fading,
until it, too, melded into the blackness of the road.

3. The Samaritan

Night had fallen …
and the man who had been robbed was still under the elm,
stretched out as if fast asleep, his head resting on the bump of a root.
A third traveler could now be seen ambling along the road.
This traveler was dressed in the simple garb of the region of Samaria,
a native, it seems, of the town of Nablus.
The Samaritan gazed at the stars while walking along the road,
only catching sight of the naked, mutilated man when nearly upon
          him.
The man, on his back, had his eyes wide open.
He merely looked up at the Samaritan helplessly, unable to say a
          word.
The Samaritan knelt down beside the man.
She immediately took the shawl from her head and covered the man
          with it.

Then she gently touched his forehead and temples with her
        fingertips,
and peered down at him with the tenderest compassion.
The man blinked his eyes, now welling with tears, and whispered.
"Thank you."
The words were lost to the air, but the Samaritan heard them.
She shook her head and, stroking his blood-matted hair, said to
        him …
"You are alive.
You are now in my care.
You have nothing more to fear.
Shhhh.…"
She wiped the tears from his cheeks with the coarse cloth of her
        sleeve,
and soothed his wounds with oil.
Helping him to his feet,
and wrapping him as best as she could in her coat,
she led him, step by step, along the road.
Though the scattered stars had come out like a million tiny
        diamonds,
no light was shed on these two people
the man who was robbed
and the good Samaritan
walking
stumbling
tripping
staggering
unseen on the road between the twin rows of dwindling poplars.

By the time the two reached an inn the dawn had broken.

Men on horseback and men in carts and men on foot overtook them
without so much as a second glance.
The people who lived by the road near the inn stared at them,
stepping back,
resting hands on the handles of their hoes, and only stopping
to chew the warm wet bread in their mouth.
The woman wore her own coat now.
She was oblivious to the stains of brown blood on it.
The man, barefoot, had only the woman's shawl to cover him.
But such attire was not unknown in the region.
Before long, not a single person was paying the least attention to
       them.
After all, this was the start of a new day,
and people had things to do.

The good Samaritan asked the innkeeper to look after the man
until he recovered from his ordeal.
She gave the innkeeper enough money to clothe, feed and shelter
       him.
She did not give her name or say the place from which she came.
But by her accent the innkeeper knew that she was a Samaritan.
"I will look after this man," he told her, as she stood at the door of
       his inn.
"But, tell me one thing, please."
"What is it?"
"What are you to this man?"
"I am nothing to him," replied the good Samaritan.
"But you cannot be nothing now," he said. "You have encountered
       him."
"Well, then, just say that I am his neighbor."

"Neighbor. Ah … neighbor. A very nice word, that."

And, as the good Samaritan shut the door of the inn behind her,
the innkeeper, holding his ample belly in both hands,
whispered to himself.
"Ah, neighbor. Neighbor. A very nice word, indeed."

4. Neighbors

From that day on,
people who lived by the side of the road
heard of the story of the good Samaritan.
And from that day on, too, they began to call each other
        "neighbors,"
no matter where along the road they lived.
People greeted people they didn't know,
and visited other people living far away, their new "neighbors."
Farmers who for centuries had tended their fields with their backs to
        the road
now turned toward it when caring for their crops.
Fruitpickers no longer buried their heads in the leaves of their trees.
And shepherds developed a method of keeping an eye on their flocks
        and the road at the same time,
although this was by no means an easy thing to do.
High priests declared "The Tale of the Good Samaritan" a miracle.
They built a church on the land by "The Sacred Elm."
Men of influence and power founded "The Loyal Society of the Elm
        Tree,"

an organization dedicated to the preservation of morality.

But as for our road,
well … it was still the same road
with its bumps and grooves,
and your standard number of potholes.
And though its scars were covered over
and the occurrences that caused them as good as forgotten,
it stretched as it always did
from one end of itself to the other.

JOSHUA

1. The Army That Accomplished Its Work By Night

This story takes place in a land flowing with milk and honey, enough
for all of the peoples living far and wide throughout it.

In the beginning, people spread themselves evenly over the land.
They formed nations according to accent and custom,
taking great care to see that everyone was looked after,
from birth to death.
At the time when Joshua came into the world
there were thirteen nations living in the land of milk and honey.
But one nation had altered the lie of the land
to hoard all of the goodness and richness for itself.
This nation had built an unassailable city
with a wall so thick and so high
that nothing made by man could penetrate it or bring it down.
This nation boasted an almighty army, too.
The army left the city in the dead of night,
stealing and pillaging anything of worth
from the other twelve peoples who lived in the land.
During the day the army took refuge in the city,
assaying its spoils
and pricing its slaves,
men and women seized from the other twelve nations,
abducted in their beds

dragged through their doors
thrown into carts at the tip of a sword
to be disposed of as it pleased the army.
The army rejoicing!
The army celebrating!
The army rampaging!
The army invincible!
The army omnipotent!
Never had the world seen such a city before,
its wealth hoarded within insurmountable walls,
safeguarded by an army that accomplished its work by night.

Now, there was not a man or woman among the other twelve nations
who did not feel hurt and wronged.
Each had lost a husband
or a wife
or a mother
or a father
or a sister
or a brother
or, worst of all that can be imagined, a child.
And each could tell you of an immense grief,
a grief whose depth cannot be plumbed,
a grief whose pain can never be soothed.
There is a bitter story for every house, tent and shelter,
the story of the loved one who was killed
or raped
or maimed
or taken away forever
by the army that accomplished its work by night.

2. The Scarlet Cord

While growing up, Joshua had heard stories of misery and suffering.
He watched in silence as mothers threw themselves to the ground,
writhing in the agony of loss,
as fathers pounded their fists against the air,
as orphaned children sat in the sand,
staring blankly into a world that was a mystery to them.
And when he became an adult,
Joshua took on this misery and suffering as his own.
He desired nothing more than for the wall to come down,
to free those people kept there against their will
and to open the city to all its roads
so that anyone, from any nation, could settle in it.

One day, after dark,
when the hooked moon had sunk beneath the horizon,
Joshua sent two trusted friends to the city on a mission.
When the two men caught sight of the city wall,
they started to crawl on their belly through the scrub,
following a light in a window cut out of the wall.
They finally came to the edge of the wall itself.
They looked up, straining their neck, both thinking the very same
        thing.
"There is nothing man-made that will destroy this wall."
Just then they heard the whispers of a voice coming directly from
        above.
It was the voice of a woman.

"Where have you come from?"
The two men stood flush with fear against the wall.
They barely dared exchange glances.
Should we answer her?
Can we trust her?
It might cause our capture and death.
We've come this far, so we have no choice
but to put ourselves in her hands.
"We are from the twelve nations," said one of them to the woman in
        the window.
Her head disappeared.
In a flash, a long scarlet cord dropped through the darkness down
        the wall.
The two men climbed up the cord and through the window,
finding themselves in a room inside the wall.
"Sit down, please," said the woman, pointing to two chairs made of
        ash.
The candle on the table was flickering in a deep slick of wax.
She lit a new candle,
boiled water,
put two cups of hot tea on the table
and told them her story.

"I was born and raised by my mother outside the city.
My father was murdered in front of us.
I was thirteen years old at the time.
The soldiers from the city tied me up and brought me here.
They crushed our little house with my mother still inside it.
I suppose she died.
When we arrived here before dawn,

I was untied and raped over and over again by the soldiers.
They drank, becoming very drunk, as they violated me.
They spoke of their plunder, which included oil that they needed.
I suppose I was just another piece of their plunder,
not a woman
not a human being
nothing but nothing.
They have used my body ever since, as if it belonged to them,
leaving a coin or two on this table as they leave.
Ah, the people who live within this wall worship their soldiers.
Their soldiers are their heroes.
Their soldiers are their saviors.
Their soldiers are their gods!
The people who live outside the wall they call
vermin
animals
beasts.
And once having called us beasts,
they treat us like beasts,
becoming beasts themselves.
And though they kill for the motive of greed,
they claim the love of freedom, peace and all humanity
as their own."

The woman stopped.
The light of the candle carried her shadow
across the floor and over the window sill.
"How old are you now?" asked one of the men.
"Thirty-eight. I have lived like this
in this room

for twenty-five years."
"Why don't you drop the scarlet cord and run away?"
"Oh, I live for the day to be away from here.
I dream only of returning to my land and living again where my
    home was,
where I can erect a grave for my mother and tend it.
But if I escape, the soldiers will catch me, torture and kill me.
I tried it once and they beat me until I was half dead.
Guards constantly patrol the perimeter of the wall.
It is a miracle that you survived unseen.
It has never happened before."

Just then there were three soft knocks at her door.
"That's a warning," she said.
"You are in danger.
Go through that opening in the ceiling and cover yourselves well
    with the flax that is there."
The two men did this,
and the woman closed the opening in the ceiling behind them,
disheveling her bed
mussing up her hair
and ripping the sleeve of her blouse.
She washed and dried one teacup,
to make it look like she was alone.

A thunder of footsteps resounded along the corridor
and soon there was loud pounding on the door.
"Open up, harlot!" shouted a soldier.
The woman walked to the door.
Panting in a display of desperation,

she flung it open, crying, "Did you see them?"

Five soldiers bolted into the room, shoving the woman aside.

"Where are they? We know there are two of them."

"Yes, they were here, it is true," she said.

"They had dressed themselves as soldiers, just like you,

so naturally I took them in.

But when I recognized by their accents that they were outsiders,

I demanded that they leave.

That is when they forced themselves on me … look at my bed.

Look at me."

"It is no more than you deserve," said one of the soldiers, kicking the
covers off her bed with his muddy boot.

"To be had by an animal."

"You must hurry," said the woman as frantically as she could.

"If you pursue them now you will overtake them."

"You have harbored outsiders," said one of the soldiers, toppling the
table.

The candle flame was snuffed before it reached the ground.

It was now pitch dark in the room.

"We will make you pay for this before too long!"

The five soldiers left the room, slamming the door behind them.

The woman lit the candle again,

stood on the table and uncovered the opening in the ceiling.

"You must leave. Go out through my window, on the scarlet cord."

And the two men did just that,

fortunately evading the patrol.

They headed for the hills,

where they hid for three days and three nights.

"It is thanks to a miracle that we have survived," said one man to the
other.

"No miracle.
It is thanks to a poor woman who, despite everything,
is still able to hope."

3. The Twelve Stones

After hiding in the hills, the two men returned to their people.
They reported to Joshua that the city was inviolable.
"The wall is as thick as two houses,
and it is patrolled constantly by armed guards.
The gate is protected night and day by half an army."
"I have a plan nonetheless," said Joshua.
"But there can be no plan," said one of the men.
"No weapon can conquer an unconquerable city."
Nevertheless Joshua left them, harboring his plan.
He called a meeting of the leaders of the other eleven nations that
          lived in the land.
And as they began to gather,
he went to the river that bordered his home,
picking twelve small equal-size stones from its bed.
He weighed them carefully to make sure that none was heavier than
          the next.
Placing them carefully in a braided salt bag,
he returned to his tent
where the other eleven leaders were waiting for him.
Joshua greeted them all with many hugs
and kisses, and they all greeted each other in this way,
which, it must be said, took up a lot of time
and was rather awkward considering the modest size of Joshua's

tent.

Then the twelve leaders of the twelve nations

sat in a circle around a colorful rug of embroidered gardens.

Each leader gave a long speech, starting with the leader to the left of
Joshua,

and ending with the leader to his right.

It was night before the eleven speeches had finally come to an end,

and Joshua summarized them in this way:

"Permit me to summarize your speeches, if I may," he said,

urging them to eat the nuts and dried fruit in pewter bowls before
them.

"'We are frightened and helpless.' Is that the gist of what you all
said?"

And the eleven leaders of the eleven nations nodded and clapped
their hands,

for Joshua had said in three seconds what had taken them the better
part of the day and evening.

Then Joshua spoke of his plan.

"I want you to return to your people," he said calmly.

"Gather them together, as many as are capable of travel,

young and old

strong and weak

dull and bright

brave and meek.

And I want you to meet me along the river that borders my home.

It is the same river that flows through our land to the city and
beyond.

I want you each to bring a trumpet and nothing else.

No weapon, nothing that can maim or kill."

"But how can we stand up to the city armed only with trumpets?"

asked one of the leaders,
moistening his full mustache with his even fuller lower lip.
"The city will be compelled to deal with us as we are," replied
        Joshua.
"What do you mean, Joshua?" asked a balding leader, grasping his
        toes.
"You will see where our strength lies, I promise you.
Now," added Joshua, "I have placed a stone beside your pewter
        bowls."
The leaders all looked at their stone.
"These represent each nation of people.
They form a circle.
Tell your people and your children that together
we form a circle that will not be broken.
We all depend on each other to complete ourselves."

And with that, Joshua bade goodbye on the bank of the river
to the eleven leaders of the eleven nations,
returned to his tent and feel fast asleep
on the colorful rug of embroidered gardens
inside the indestructible circle of stones.

4. The Battle

The day of the battle finally arrived.
Thousands upon thousands of people made their way,
along the river that bordered Joshua's home
to the walled city.
The eleven leaders of the eleven nations each held a trumpet,

as instructed by Joshua.
Joshua had further directed the people to form a circle
around the wall of the city,
person by person
family by family
village by village
nation by nation.
And when they had done this,
Joshua passed word along,
all the way from one end of the wall to the other and back again,
for the leaders, upon his signal,
to sound their trumpets.
The soldiers outside and inside, on top and below,
were amused, not threatened, by the circle around them.
"Oh, look," hollered a guard above the massive gate.
"They have brought their grandfathers and their toddlers to fight
          us."
"See that trumpet!" yelled a soldier at the very top of the wall.
"Oh, I tremble in my boots!"
"Well, blow me down!" shouted the soldier next to him.
And the soldiers within earshot guffawed so raucously
that their helmets went skitting down the wall.

At that, Joshua put his trumpet to his lips
and played a single long loud clear note.
Immediately this note was sounded, trumpet by trumpet,
all the way around the wall.
Now the guards and soldiers on top and below, inside and outside,
began to jeer angrily from their stations.
They jeered at the thousands upon thousands of people surrounding

them.
They jeered at their leaders who dared to threaten them with sound.
And you could tell from the mad tone of their jeering
that before long they would come down and out, to rush the circle
to break it
to cut it down
to decimate it
to slaughter all those who stood their ground in it.

Joshua knew that this was his single moment.
"Let all of the peoples of the land shout!" he cried.
"Shout, shout and shout with all your might.
Shout for your lives, to make the future bright."
And, as word passed around the circle that surrounded the wall,
all of the people of the twelve nations began to shout.
Men in their eighties raised their voice
young women bellowed
toddlers hooted
and infants at their mother's breast cried out,
though they hardly needed prompting to cry out at any time of the
        day or night.
As the shouting rose and rose,
its deafening roar shook the very Earth.
And the soldiers below and above, inside and out
put their hands under their helmets and covered their ears.
With mouths contorted and eyes open in awe,
they tried to defend themselves as best as they knew how,
flailing arms
cursing threats
threatening harm

swishing swords in the air,
to sever the flow of sound and breath that was coming at them
like a wall.
But there was no defense against sound in the air,
the sound of the voices of all the people
who formed a complete circle around the city.

And before their moon-like eyes
on the backdrop of a pitch-black sky,
the wall itself began to groan and rumble,
the great wall that had been insurmountable
unassailable
impenetrable
the great wall defended by the army that worshipped the night.
And as it came down,
it crushed the army above and below, inside and out.
It was as if the wall itself was taking revenge on its protectors.
But just before the wall itself crumbled into countless pieces,
a long scarlet cord appeared in a window,
then the shadow,
then the figure of a woman in a dress decorated in the blue flowers
        of the flax from which it was made.
She planted her feet firmly on the ground outside the wall.
She wrapped the scarlet cord around her.
She went up to Joshua,
bowed her head once,
and, smiling a gracious smile,
passed him,
walking in the direction of her home.

After that, the slaves were freed
and families throughout the land were reunited.
The peoples of the twelve nations moved into the city.
Well, not all of them.
Not everybody likes to live in a big city.

As to what happened to all the stolen treasures in the city,
the silver and gold,
the vessels of bronze and iron,
and as to whether the wall around the city was rebuilt
in the land flowing with milk and honey …
that's really another story.

It's not for me to say.

JOSEPH

1. Dreams

Joseph belonged to Potiphar.

Now, people living in our day and age might find this sentence
      strange.
Not the words themselves.
Lovers say they belong to each other.
Members of groups proclaim their belonging with pride.
People give themselves, heart and body, to a country.
We affirm loyalty to some thing.
We swear dependency on someone.
But Joseph really *belonged* to Potiphar.
That is, Potiphar owned Joseph, as a man owns a piece of luggage
or a woman, a pair of leather boots.
Imagine being controlled by somebody else. Imagine it!
Your present thoughts and future dreams
your every move and gesture
the sounds you make
your time awake, your very sleep
dreams you may only half remember
desires you may not fully understand yourself …
all these things will belong to your owner.
You are not yours.
You are somebody else's.

Joseph would not have fallen into such hands
had it not been for his dreams.
It was his dreams that sealed his fate.

Joseph was a shy young man.
His timidity was often mistaken for arrogance.
This nature of misunderstanding befalls shy people,
particularly those who voice their inner thoughts in unconventional
      ways.
Revealing your dreams is one of those ways.
People may misinterpret and guard themselves against the dreams
      of others.
They misconceive vision as intent,
as if vision is a mask for the mechanics of design.

Anyway, this is how Joseph's fate was sealed.
One morning, while sitting around the breakfast table with his
      brothers and parents, Joseph said …
"Pass the bread."
And while his mother reached across the smoothly polished ebony
      table,
he went on to relate his dream of the previous night.
"We were all in the field, harvesting the wheat,
the waning moon a half-eaten melon overhead,
the morning sun, a glowing fire on the horizon,
when the sheaves that you, my brothers, had tied,
formed a circle around my sheaf,
stood on end
and bowed down low.

Thank you, mother. Now, the butter, please."
Joseph's father pushed the butter dish along the table with his index
    finger.
"Isn't that funny?" asked Joseph, gazing around the table.
Neither his brothers nor his parents were saying a word.
But it was obvious from their pained expressions that they were not
    amused by the content of this dream.
"What's the matter? Can't I have another piece of bread and butter?"
It was plain to everyone there except Joseph
that bread and butter had nothing to do with the silence at the table.
"That wasn't all," added Joseph, enthusiastically,
licking his lips as he spread butter over his bread.
"The next thing I knew a dense flock of magpies was flying
    overhead,
pulling a black curtain attached to their tails right across the sky.
And on the curtain hung that half-eaten moon, suddenly radiant,
and the sun, an enormous orange without its peel, beside it
and more stars than come out in a thousand nights.
Oh, this butter is good. Is it freshly churned?"
He looked to his mother, who in turn looked to his father.
There was another silence at the table, longer than the one before.
Joseph chewed his bread, swallowed it in a lump, and continued.
"And then the moon, the sun and all the stars flickered and twinkled
    in harmony,
as I waved my arms in a signal to the high heavens.
Isn't that funny too?"
Joseph smiled a big smile,
wiping a smear of butter from his lower lip with his knuckles.
Joseph's brothers were staring at their father,
who now had his elbows on the table and his head in his hands.

"What's the matter?" asked Joseph.
Again neither Joseph's brothers nor parents would say a word.
But it was obvious from the crossed lines of distress on their face
that they were repelled by Joseph's confessions.

Sometimes it doesn't pay to tell other people your dreams,
especially when the threads of your wishes are intertwined with
        theirs.
Joseph finished eating,
excused himself from the table
and went outside to talk to his goats.

2. The Slave

Joseph's brothers saw his dream as a plot
to lord himself over them.
So, one day they grabbed Joseph and threw him down a dry well.
They wanted to be rid of him forever.
It was, by all rights, a pretty drastic thing to do to someone over a
        dream.
But there was more to it than that, as you can imagine.
The brothers were jealous of Joseph, who was their father's favorite
        son.
Maybe their intent was to kill something in their father
by murdering their brother.
Even so, it didn't end there.

A group of well-to-do traders happened to be passing through the
        region,

and catching sight of them gave the brothers second thoughts,
second thoughts that harbored a more appealing idea.
Acting upon these thoughts,
they drew Joseph from the well
and sold him to the traders.
After all, they reasoned, he is our brother
and he must be worth something.
Besides, when all is said and done,
it's easier to have a slave brother than a dead brother on your
        conscience.
And, so long as their father believed that Joseph was dead,
the overall effect would be the same.
They would have the best of both worlds!
So they tore Joseph's robe to strips and shreds,
slaughtered one of his goats,
soaked the robe in its blood
and hurried home to offer it to their parents.
"Look, father, look, mother," they said, holding out the bloody robe,
as children do with something they have proudly made.
"Joseph has been eaten up by a wild animal."
Joseph's brothers shed streamy crocodile tears,
which mingled with the real tears of their parents.
Joseph's mother and father were stunned into silence,
condemned by their own sons,
and sentenced to an imprisonment of unending grief.

As for those sons …
well, that night, snugly wrapped in soft fleece blankets,
they chuckled under their breath and giggled uncontrollably.
With the brother they called "The Dreamer" gone

they would sleep soundly, night after night,
untroubled by visions of their own
or anyone else's creation.

As for Joseph, he had found himself standing upright, naked,
trembling and shivering on the bed of a dry well,
his legs and sides scraped, scratched and trickling in blood.
He had no idea in the world
why his brothers would have dropped him down there.
"Perhaps it is some kind of prank," he thought.
Ever since he was a little boy,
he had mistaken his brothers' viciousness for sport.
"HELP!" he cried.
"Someone, anyone, please come and save me!"
But no one came that night.
Joseph slept with his head resting against the jagged stones of the
     well,
dreaming of nothing but going home to his parents and brothers.
He was awakened by voices that he immediately recognized.
"Help me! I'm sorry if I hurt you!" he cried up to the little round of
     light.
A thick knotted rope appeared, jiggling in front of his face.
He grabbed the rope and held to it with all his might.
As Joseph ascended,
his knees and buttocks banged against sharp stones.
But, despite the pain that he felt, he was smiling.
He wanted nothing more than to apologize to his brothers
for giving them offense.
The first thing Joseph saw when his head popped out of the well's
     mouth

was his brothers' open hands.
He squinted, gazing at the bright morning light through a net of
    fingers.
The next thing he knew a clean white linen robe was wound around
    him.
"Thank you," he said to his brothers.
"I'm sorry to be such a nuisance to you all the time."
Without saying a word to Joseph,
the brothers pushed and pulled him toward a caravan of traders.
In a matter of minutes Joseph was riding atop a camel,
its flanks draped in multicolored bags that bulged with spices and
    resins.
Joseph waved goodbye to his brothers,
who, nonetheless, had turned their back on him for their journey
    home.

Joseph was taken to the city.
Being tall, muscular and pleasingly obedient
he was sold directly into the palace guard.
The captain of the guard, Potiphar, took an immediate liking to the
    youth.
He trained Joseph rigorously and said to him …
"I am putting you in charge of all of my possessions."
Joseph was deeply flattered by this offer of trust.
He wanted nothing more than to go home then and there
to tell his parents and brothers of his good fortune.
But, being a slave, his life was not his own.
He had to do the bidding of his owner,
whatever that owner might demand of him.

Now, Potiphar, a man of high rank and responsibility,
was frequently called away to prosecute his king's wars.
At those times, all of the other slaves and servants
were happy to follow Joseph's lead.
They saw him as no threat,
for Joseph was a meek and unassuming man
who coveted nothing that belonged to others.
What is generally seen as weakness in other men was Joseph's
strength.

One evening Potiphar's beautiful wife came to Joseph.
Joseph had just finished cleaning the captain's latrines.
"I want you to come with me," she said.
She laid her gentle hand on Joseph's shoulder.
Joseph naturally complied,
for Joseph belonged to Potiphar
and was slave to everything under his roof.
Potiphar's wife led Joseph to her private chamber, where a hot bath
had been drawn.
The steam was fragrant with sliced citrons and honey that had been
mixed into the water.
"I want you to assist me in my bath," said Potiphar's wife,
dropping her delicate gown to the floor.
Joseph, being a slave, had been used to seeing the captain's
concubines without a stitch of clothing on them.
Slaves were less than human.
Their eyes were not men's or women's eyes.
Their desires were not theirs to pursue,
their dreams not theirs to believe.
The concubines paraded naked in front of the dogs of the household

as they did before its slaves.

But Potiphar's wife had never taken her clothes off in front of Joseph.

He had been unaware that she had often stared at him as he went
about his chores.

"Come close to me," she said.

She was standing at the bath's edge with her hands on her hips.

"I … I am filthy from the latrines," said Joseph, lowering his gaze.

"Look at me," she said.

Joseph obeyed, gradually looking up her legs to her hips.

Potiphar's wife turned around.

"You may take off your robe, Joseph," she said. "I am not facing you
now."

Joseph was in a real predicament.

On the one hand he was a slave, stripped of will and personal desire.

On the other, he was his master's possession.

Not having had experience in these matters, it nevertheless occurred
to him

that his master might not approve of his entering a bath that also
had his wife in it.

"What are you waiting for?" she said.

"I want you in the bath next to me.

I want you to rub honey and citron all over my skin."

Joseph instinctively stepped backward toward the door.

All he could say was, "I … I … I … I…."

Potiphar's wife turned toward him again and approached him,

leaving wet footprints on the marble floor.

Joseph's back was now flat against the chamber door.

Potiphar's wife pressed herself against him,

taking his hands and bringing them around her waist.

She whispered, "Then come to bed with me."

She opened his robe and kissed his chest, lowering her hand and
        placing it on …
Joseph shrieked, "I cannot!
Some things are sacred, even for a slave!"
He pried himself away from her and shot out of the door.
Incensed more by his rejection than his disobedience,
Potiphar's wife grabbed the tail of his robe as he ran from her.
This caused the robe to fall from Joseph's body.
Joseph was forced to scurry down the corridor clothed only in his
        loincloth.
Potiphar's wife screamed out at the top of her lungs.
"Stop him! Stop Joseph! He has tried to rape me!"
The servants came immediately, for they were never far away,
and seeing Potiphar's wife hold out Joseph's robe,
chased after him, yelling.
"Stop, you bastard!
Stop, you despicable slave!"

When the captain returned from the battlefield,
and heard the weeping story from his wife,
he wasted no time in having Joseph arrested and thrown into prison.
Joseph found himself in the company of common thieves
and uncommon murderers.
Even those lowly humans looked down on Joseph and treated him
        with barbarity,
needling and tormenting him
hollering into his ears when he was just falling asleep
filching his food and fouling his water …
until one morning everything changed in Joseph's cell,
and his fate, if you will, turned a corner.

Fate does have corners, you know,
though they are often unseen until you are upon them.

3. Freedom

The light coming through the little window high on the cell wall
reminded Joseph of the glare in the mouth of the well,
and he sang in a whisper to himself.

Round light
Square light
Light that leads away
Round light
Square light
Come what may.
Round light
Square light
Light that makes you free
Round light
Square light
Be what you can be.

Joseph gazed around the cell.
The other prisoners were fast asleep.
Out of the blue,
a gigantic cockroach dashed across the floor and paused in the
        corner.
Joseph approached the corner on tiptoes.

He bent down and, in a single deft sweep of his hand,
captured the cockroach.
He peered through his half-open fingers
as it wriggled and butted, wriggled and butted.
Joseph then flung his captive, with great force, up toward the
        window.
It landed on the ledge and turned to Joseph, as if to address him!
But then, swiveling about, it disappeared out the window and into
        the light,
casting an eagle's shadow across the walls of the cell.
At that instant, all of the prisoners began to moan in unison.
Something had awakened them.
What was it?
Was it the morning light that now flowed through the window like a
        stream of honey?
Was it the flapping of the cockroach's wings against the streaming
        light?
Or was it something that the men saw in the mind,
something that had disturbed them
prompting them to howl softly?
"I have had a dream," said one.
"I have had one too," said another.
"And me."
"And me."
They had all dreamt detailed and drawn-out stories,
profoundly unsettling and puzzling,
in the time it took a cockroach to disappear
through a honey-colored window.

In each dream there was a common element.

That element was the number three:
three branches
three baskets of bread
three little children waiting at the end of a road.
And Joseph knew at once the meaning hidden in the dreams.
"You will all be free in three days' time," he said,
patting them individually on the shoulder and smiling benignly.
"But why?" they asked.
"I don't know that one," Joseph confessed.
"I just interpret dreams.
I can't explain people's motivations."
That was the truth.
Joseph had no talent whatsoever for explaining the whims
and illogical vagaries of human nature.
He was simply a dreamer,
a dreamer if there ever was one.

Well, it came about as Joseph had predicted.
Three days later the king freed the prisoners.
Joseph, too, was freed.
The king was informed of his rare ability,
and being a bit of a dreamer himself,
released Joseph from the bondage of slavery.
Joseph no longer belonged to Potiphar
and, in any case, had never belonged to Potiphar's wife.
Subsequently, Joseph turned further corners of fate,
the last of which led him to the path of high office.

It is said that the meek inherit the Earth.
Perhaps the best illustration of this saying is the life of Joseph.

He was an honest man who, in his years,
journeyed against the stream of light.

And though he lived a long life and traveled far,
and witnessed a myriad of wondrous events,
his heart always lacked ambition, as it was devoid of greed.

And he dreamt of only one thing …
returning home to his mother and father,
and his brothers,
all of whom he loved with an undying love.

ESTHER

1. How Esther Came to the Palace

Esther created happiness
and this is the story of how she did it.

She would not have been able to accomplish such a rare and
        wonderful feat
had it not been for the Ruler
and the ruthless men who surrounded him day and night.

Now, this Ruler reveled in the cruelest acts.
Any person
young or old
male or female
who stood between him and the aggrandizement of his stature
was arrested,
held "at the Ruler's pleasure,"
and, more often than not, executed.
For those he took to be enemies
he had erected ten gallows, each twenty meters in height
in the very center of the city.
These ten gallows came to be known as "Death Row,"
and so eager was the public to be on hand as ten necks
of ten "vicious enemies of our nation" were simultaneously
snapped

(the Ruler was a stickler for timing)
that, by and by, bleachers were built and tickets, sold
for the timely spectacle.
Gallows-side seats were reserved exclusively for the VIPs,
which stood for "Very Important Priests,"
while other seats with unimpeded views
went to relatives and trusted friends in the Ruler's inner circle.
Seats in the bleachers were up for grabs from reputable ticket
        agencies or scalpers,
the latter merciless in charging an arm and a leg
for a bird's-eye view
of the hangings.

Now, the Ruler was known far and wide for his wanton passion for
        luxury
and his need to possess a woman to do his every bidding.
His lovely wife had been just such a woman,
and he had been as content as he could ever be with her.
But a single thing changed all this.

The Ruler was fond of holding lavish state banquets
in honor of foreign dignitaries who paid obeisance to his nation.
During one such banquet,
attended on the official lawn
by kings and rooks and pawns
army chiefs and financiers
and diplomats who fawn,
the Ruler sent his Decree Secretary into the palace to fetch his wife.
The Ruler was showing off treasures acquired from unfriendly
        nations.

He wanted to display his wife as well,
for he was as proud of her as he was of anything else that was his.
But the Decree Secretary returned to the banquet on the lawn
empty handed.
"Where is my wife?
What is the meaning of this?" demanded the Ruler.
"She will not come, sir," he said, lowering his long neck.
Several Very Important Priests scurried across the carefully edged
      lawn.
"Sir," intoned one, "you must not let this pass. It will set a precedent."
"A man must put his foot down," piped in another,
"even if it crushes the head of one he may care for.
If he doesn't, she will never obey him
and he will cease to be lord in his own house."
"You must not let sentiment rule your heart," advised a third.
And, in unison, they counseled him to do away with his wife,
which he did the next morning, in secret, by flinging her off a cliff
after the kings and rooks and pawns
the army chiefs and financiers
and the diplomats who fawn
were gone.
And the Decree Secretary dutifully read out the decree
proclaiming that something "untoward"
had befallen the wife of the Ruler and that she was no longer with us.
Among people in the know of what had "befallen" her,
this decree came to be known as "The Decree of Lethal Rejection."
This all left the Ruler in a state of sentimental disarray,
for he needed a living object to adore alongside his precious objects.
So he sent out his official scouts
to scour the land for a suitable young woman.

It wasn't long before a few hundred
had been rounded up and readied.
These young women, from nations far and wide,
were all striking in their beauty.
But none was so strikingly beautiful as Esther,
who came from across the border.
Her people were considered by the Ruler to be his most detested
        enemy.
Some years previous to this, he had conquered them.
Esther's mother and father had been among the ordinary people
whose house had been reduced to dust with them in it.
Esther, only a child then, had crawled from under the crumbled
        house.
She had been adopted by a cousin whose name was Mordecai.
Mordecai had looked after her
until the night that the Ruler's scouts broke into his house
and whisked her away.
After that Mordecai crossed the border
and moved into the city, to be close to the Ruler's palace,
making it a point to visit it every day.
He wanted to keep an eye on Esther.

The Ruler craved public adoration
(After all, hadn't he erected ten awesome gallows for their
        amusement?)
opening the palace doors every day,
allowing all to share with him the distended joys of his fancies.
Every day religiously
Mordecai made his way to the palace,
and every day he took the grand tour of the Ruler's riches

that represented the cultures of all of the lands he had invaded.
Before long Mordecai came to be on intimate terms with the guards,
joking
gambling
and drinking with them
as if he was one of their number.

In the meantime
the Ruler had become smitten by Esther
who was as gentle and clever as she was beautiful.
The Ruler did not know anything about her.
Her person was not his concern.
He ruled without a care for people's nature.
His only care was for blissful display:
the blissful display of power
the blissful display of wealth
the blissful display of how to subjugate
by stealth.

So Esther became the Ruler's wife,
and a decree was issued throughout the land
that all should recognize her as such.
The Ruler, for his part, was ever indifferent
to where Esther had begun her life
and to the kind of woman, deep down, she was.

2. Schemes And Plots

Esther was not afraid of the Ruler.

This alone set her apart from those in his circle.
She went to see him without being summoned.
She told him what she thought about this and that.
She even made him dismantle the ten gallows
that loomed over the center of the city.
This, in particular, caused the Ruler to sulk,
for he was inordinately fond of doing away with undesirable people.
"What a waste of a good gallows," he whispered to himself, adding
          to her …
"I am a new man, though, thanks to you."
Assuring his wife that he had mended his brutal ways,
he transported his prisoners by the cartload across the border,
where they were held, tortured and hacked to death.
He told her, "I am killing no one in this country."
Slapping his palms together as if brushing them of ashes,
he told the men who surround him, "It is out of my hands."
As for that inner circle, some among them,
led by a Very Important Priest named Hamon,
were bitter and unhappy.
"Thanks to *that* woman, our Ruler has become soft and expendable,"
          said Hamon to his co-conspirator, General Peneneus.
"He who was once a god to us is now but an annoying shadow."
The two men schemed and plotted to murder the Ruler
and lay the blame,
in the shape of a curved blood-stained dagger,
at the feet of Esther.

Now it just so happened that at this time
Mordecai often played Pharaoh, a popular card game,
with some of the guards at the palace.

It was here that he became privy to the rumor
that there were schemes and plots against the Ruler.
When the game was over, the guards retired,
and Mordecai made his way to the inner rooms.
He knocked on Esther's door.
"Esther, Esther," he called in a low voice.
"Who's there?" she asked.
"It's me, Mordecai. I must see you."
"Oh, Mordecai," she said, opening the door.
He whirled in and bolted the door.
He told her of the plot against her husband.
"It must be Hamon," she said to herself, after Mordecai left.
"It can only be Hamon. He alone craves power more than my
        husband."

The Ruler was ecstatic to be visited that night by Esther.
But the news of the plot dampened his mood,
turning his passion for her into a lust for revenge.
He stormed out of his chamber,
summoning all of the guards from their sleep.
He lined them up and spoke to them.
"I give you all the opportunity to live to see tomorrow's dawn.
Tell me, any one of you, who is plotting against me.
If none of you speaks, you will all be carted across the border
in the dead of this very night
tortured
and pulled apart
like a parboiled cat."
One of the guards who had been playing Pharaoh spoke up.
"Sir, I cannot say for sure, for there are only wild rumors about,

but a man named Mordecai, who frequents the palace
did seem to have some knowledge of these schemes and plots."
The Ruler did not know Mordecai from Adam.
He nonetheless called for his trusted priest, Hamon.
Hamon wasted no time in sending soldiers to Mordecai's home,
seized him
and clamped him in thick rusted irons
in his own little private dungeon.

As the day was dawning Hamon returned home,
awakened his wife and said to her …
"Good morning, my darling.
Shhh. Do not look so alarmed.
Soon you will be sleeping in a more sumptuous bed.
Your body will be crawling with gold and jewels."
And he lay beside her and fell promptly to sleep,
for nothing exhausts a man
like the prospect
of a good assassination.

Things moved swiftly after that,
as they often do in these ancient stories.
Esther discovered her cousin Mordecai's whereabouts,
freed him
and informed her husband
who his true enemy was.
The Ruler sent his guards to Hamon's house.
Hamon was captured in the middle of a dream,
just like thousands of the people he had condemned.
He was immediately escorted across the border.

There executioners,
paid a decent living wage by the Ruler,
tore his four limbs from his body with their gloved hands,
put the bits and pieces into a large hemp bag
and tossed the bag and all that was left of Hamon
down a black bottomless pit.

"It's out of my hands," announced the Ruler to Esther,
once again dusting off his palms.
"But no, he isn't," she said.
"Oh yes he is. He's fallen into the Earth, never to return."
"But," she cried to him, "don't you see?"
"See what?"
"The brutalities that you commit are no better than those that others
        would commit against you!"

No one had ever spoken to the Ruler like this before.
The Ruler had surrounded himself with people who agreed with his
        every word.
(The most shrewd among them had put words into his mouth before
        agreeing with them.)
"How can I subdue my enemies if I do not kill a lot of them?" he
        asked in all innocence.
"By understanding them," replied Esther,
holding his hand in hers
and stroking the soft hairs that grew around his knuckles.
"Understanding them? What do you mean?" he asked,
resting his head on her shoulder.
"Listen to them.
Feel what they feel.

Listen again
and provide for them."

It was at that very tender moment,
probably the tenderest that had ever passed between them,
that Esther told him of her origins.
It confused the Ruler no end that he could so deeply love
a woman who belonged to a people that he hated so passionately.
He looked into her light emerald eyes
as if the answer to his confusion could be found in them.

Esther's eyes sparkled into his.
She took his head in her hands
and brought it close to her.
The Ruler wept,
as much for himself
as for all the people whose life
he had extinguished.

3. The Steps of the Palace at Dawn

You might have thought that Mordecai
of all people
would have been satisfied with these turns of event.
For one thing, he was rewarded for his loyalty with a vast mansion
servants
a fortune in gold
and, most valuable of all,
a new status that put him above reproach.

But Mordecai was a man burning with unfulfilled desire.
He wanted territory and greater wealth for his people
who lived across the border,
as their "superior nature " (these are Mordecai's words) demanded.
Protected by the Ruler and his own new status,
he crossed the border many times,
fomenting discontent
revolt
and insurrection.
He brought under his sway
the very torturers and executioners in his own country
who had done the Ruler's work for him.
He gathered a small but disciplined army in the Ruler's country
from among soldiers loyal to General Peneneus,
the army chief who had served as Hamon's right hand.
And when he felt the time was ripe for a move,
he went to the palace
to elicit the support of his cousin,
Esther,
whom he had brought up
as his own daughter.
"She is one of us," he thought.
"She will fall behind me.
She will be our queen.
Queen Esther …
Queen of *our* Nation!"

Night fell as Mordecai entered the palace rooms
to tell Esther of the plot against her husband,

just as he had done once before.
Esther greeted Mordecai with a warm embrace.
"I will not stay long," he said, folding his velvet robe over his knees.
"I have come to warn you of a plot against the Ruler."
"That is impossible!" she exclaimed.
"My husband is now loved by our people.
No one in his right mind would think of murdering him."
Mordecai paused.
He approached Esther
and laid a heavy palm on her shoulder.
"I am the one who would murder him."
"You?!"
"Yes, but listen!
Esther, listen to me!
It is for *our* people, Esther.
These are not your people, Esther.
These are enemies of your people, Esther.
Your own people are crying out for revenge and justice, Esther.
You must be true to your own.
Esther!"
Mordecai left, to carry out preparations for the final blow
on the steps of the palace at dawn.

What was Esther to do?
She was trapped between two loyalties:
one to the people she now lived among
and the other to the people who had given her life.

The night sky grew pale
and the stars, save for the brightest, faded into it.

When the brightest stars, too, gradually vanished,
as if painted out of the sky,
all that was left was Venus
radiant and white,
rocking as if on a hook
above the horizon.

Finally Mordecai arrived at the palace steps
shoulder to shoulder with his general.
At the rear marched a small army under their command.
The Ruler was there to meet him,
with Esther by his side.
The dull yellow light of the morning sun rolled over the army,
striking Esther full on.
She appeared to all
as a marble statue
as tall as a pillar
at the very top of the palace steps.
"Come down those steps!" ordered General Peneneus.
"If you come peacefully, there will be no need to spill the blood of
        our people."
"Mordecai!" shouted Esther over the heads of the soldiers.
"Mordecai! You must leave this country now,
and take these soldiers with you.
You will be given safe passage across the border.
I promise that to you."
Mordecai stood among the soldiers,
his purple velvet sleeves brushing against his polished brassards.
"My country is your country too, Esther," he hollered.
"My people are your people.

It is you who are betraying them, Esther!"
"No, Mordecai. It is you who betray all people.
There will be no more bloodshed!
Someone must come along and say 'STOP!'
If that someone be a woman like me,
then all the more power to me!"
Taking this as a challenge,
the general raised his massive sword high into the air.
The soldiers gripped their swords in their fists.
Their muscles grew taut.
Even the air stood still
as the soldiers prepared to storm the steps,
running through anyone,
man or woman,
who dared stand in their way.

But just then …
people stepped out from behind the pillars of the palace,
ordinary men and women,
armed with clubs and knives and scythes.
General Peneneus laughed a belly laugh,
and his men laughed heartily with him.
"Is this the army that the Ruler musters against me?
Paltry citizens with homemade weapons?"
The air stirred,
as the soldiers drew their swords,
waving them like flags
cutting through light and shadow,
eclipsing the sun that shone on Esther …
when thousands of men and women appeared

in front of them
behind them
to the left
and to the right of them.
There was no place left to stand.
People now occupied all the ground in the center of the city,
where once a row of gallows had seemed to reach to the high heavens.

"We will allow you to leave," said Esther.
"You, Mordecai, raised me.
You gave me the chance to live my life.
I cannot take the same away from you."
Mordecai looked about.
"Very well, Esther," he cried. "I will do what you say."
And he marched through the mass of people,
followed by his general and their small army of soldiers.
They marched over the ground where the tall gallows had been.
They marched through the city and out its gates.
They marched by rivers and farmland and woods and hills …
and continued marching,
with scowling faces,
with knuckles as white as fire,
until they crossed the border
into Esther's old country.

What had changed the Ruler so completely?
How did a man who executed innocent people so gleefully
come to treat all people now with compassion and forgiveness?

It was thanks to Esther,

who taught him to be like her.

The Ruler died not long after that
and Esther became the new leader.

As it stood,
her two countries
were not at war …
nor, however, were they at peace.

Esther, for one,
was not going to let anything come between them
so long as there was the breath of life
left in her.

THE STORY OF ADAM AND EVE
—Narrated by a Snake

1. To Begin With

To begin with, I don't understand
how I came to be seen as a symbol of Evil.
To be honest, I myself wouldn't wish such a thing
on any person
fish
reptile
and not even on a frog
though, even I must admit, that's stretching it.
And please don't say, "These things happen."
Nothing "happens."
Everything exists only in the way it is told.
Call somebody or something "Evil" and "It's Evil."
Call them "Good" and "They're Good."

So, it is high time, if you ask me
to set the record straight once and for all.
Time to peel the skin of falsity away from myth.
Time to remove the venom of envy from the tongue.
Time to infuse "all the joy of the snake" into life itself.

Time to return to the very beginning of time ....

In the beginning there was nothing
or so I genuinely believe.
Then, in a matter of days
seven to be exact
the Earth as we know it came into being.
If you believe this already
there is no need to read here further.
If you doubt this now
I urge you to follow me to the end.

First, allow me to establish my credentials.
I was there—or here, if you will—at the beginning.
Well, not right at the very beginning.
Nobody was here then.
There was just total darkness
then clear light
then a hell of a sea of water
then lots and lots of land and
a whole bunch of weeds, bushes and trees to cover it up.
After that, the four seasons came into being
cutting straight across the face of the Earth.

Another day passed and fish were swarming in the seas
busily looking for other fish that resembled them.
The birds and the bees suddenly flew through the air
flapping frantically
seeking out other birds and bees.
That was what basically started it all in motion.
So, if you want to blame somebody for the state of the world today
blame it on the birds and the bees.

For Heaven's sake, don't blame it on the snakes!

That night, the stars came out
and all the creatures of the air marveled at them.
Some of them tried to fly all the way up to the stars.
But they soon found that no matter how high they flew
the stars got no closer, and not even a twinkle brighter.
Some of the birds, such as the nighthawk, flew so high
that the breath of life was sucked right out of them.
Their wings collapsed tightly around them
and, shuddering, they dropped like shadows to the Earth.
The ones that landed in water were immediately devoured
and the ones that fell to the ground lay where they fell
until ants appeared the next day
enveloping them in the black cloak of their bodies.

That night, all of the creatures in the air and the sea
were frightened for their lives.
This is because they had only been in existence for the one day.
Who knew that the Sun was going to come up again?
And in the same spot that it had come up the day before
(which came to be known, for the first time, as "yesterday").
Who knew that life would go on?
It might have ended with the darkness
for all they knew.

That very first night, the birds created Constellations.
They imagined timid bird hunters and fearless bird heroes in the sky.
And they created stories of these feathered heroes
unaware that this would someday help their offspring

find bearings in the sky.
Without stories, birds
like snakes
and humans alike
are lost.

Before anybody knew it …
for, after all, there was still nobody there who could know it …
five of the seven days had been taken up.
There were still no snakes
no humans
and not even any frogs worth mentioning
(not that frogs are worth mentioning).
The Sun was about to come up again
in the same spot it had come up the day before.

And that is how the Fifth Day ended in the Garden of Eden.

2. The Sudden Population Explosion in the Garden of Eden

It was a quiet morning in the Garden of Eden.
Flies and mosquitoes were hectically multiplying in pools and
    ditches,
their whirr and buzz mingling with the soft rustle
on the straight and curved branches of the trees.
And though there was a Moon in the sky
the Moon was but a day or two old itself
and wouldn't be visible till that day gave in to night.

How big was the Garden of Eden?
Why, it stretched all the way around the Earth and back again.
There wasn't a star in the entire Universe
that you couldn't see in the night skies of the Garden of Eden.

On the Sixth Day
the Sun had barely time to nudge over the horizon
when creatures of all shapes
sizes
and colors
began roaming, hopping, rolling and crawling
foaming, creeping, whimpering and calling
growling, bellowing, slithering and bawling
over and under and inside every bit of soil and sand under the Sun.
You might think this would transform the Garden of Eden
into a very crowded garden, indeed.
In actuality
the Garden of Eden had elbow room, so to speak, for all Creation.
Every creature had its place
though some creatures desired the places of others.
No sooner had they set foot, or whatever they set, on the land
than did they start to fight.
Some just pretended to fight
while others fought to the death.
Some gave others the cold shoulder or whatever
while some attached themselves to others, entirely uninvited,
making a good living out of the association.

And even though the Garden of Eden knew the strong and the weak

the fit and the lame
the wronged
the meek
the wild and the tame …
not one creature thought itself superior to any other.
(Names like "Rex" came much much later.)

As of morning on the Sixth Day in the Garden of Eden
harmony reigned throughout the land, seas and sky.
Friendliness? Not really.
Harmony doesn't require everybody to be friendly.
You see, despite some pretty old rumors,
Paradise was not a particularly friendly place.
"Harmonious" is the word that describes it best.

Harmonious is the best you can expect from a Garden of Eden.

3. The Meeting Under the Apple Tree

Now, the Garden of Eden was not a quiet place.
Every minute of that day brought new noises to it.
The animals hooted and neighed
screeched and lowed
beeped and bayed
squeaked and meowed.
But once out in space
these sounds merged into a single continuous note:
the first earthly music made in the Garden of Eden.

As I said a moment ago
not one creature looked upon itself
as superior to any other.
Not, that is, until humans
made their appearance
in the Garden of Eden.
Humans saw themselves as different from all the others
and that is what led,
not any snake, I tell you,
to the creation of Evil.
If humans later blamed it on me
it just goes to show
what I said moments ago:
"Everything exists only in the way it is told."

It was this Evil that turned the harmony of the Garden of Eden
to disarray
to disorder
and to utter disaster.

Here's how Adam and Eve found themselves under an apple tree.
This time I was there
to witness it all.

A man who already had a name for himself
stood naked and alone in the shade of the tree.
He called himself "Adam."
The ground was blanketed with juicy red apples
yet the tree, too, was bulging with apples.
You couldn't see the leaves for the apples.

Such was abundance in the Garden of Eden.

By the time the Sun had climbed above the canopy of green
Adam had cleared the space below the tree
of fallen apples, flowers, grasses and weeds.
He had pushed in the walls of a little pool below there
burying the catfish and the little turtles in mud.
He had picked up a piglet that had strayed by
gripped it by its hind legs and smashed its head to bits
against the sturdy trunk of the tree.
This shook the tree of more of its apples.
Yet strange as it may seem
even though many more apples fell to the ground
some of them striking Adam on the head
there was still the same number of apples left in the tree.

"Damn it all!" hollered Adam.
He clenched his fists into the sky
and kicked all the apples out of his way.
These were the first earthly words spoken in the Garden of Eden.

Adam now rested against the trunk of the apple tree.
It was cool there
and he wiped his brow of sweat.
For he had worked hard
in those first moments of life.
He looked around his little patch of the Garden of Eden
and smiled generously to himself.

 As for me, well, I was right above Adam

coiled around the trunk.
He did not see me.
My skin was the dark color of bark.
I felt myself a part of the tree itself.

Suddenly Adam felt a pain in his belly.
He did not know at first what was causing this pain.
With his left hand he grabbed an apple.
With his right hand he ripped flesh
from the shattered body of the piglet.
He put his left hand in his mouth
then his right hand.
Left, apple
right, piglet …
until the pain in his belly was gone.
Again he smiled to himself
pushing the remains of the apple and piglet
with the bare soles of his feet
outside the shadowed circle.

When the Sun sat straight up at the top of the sky
Adam felt another, sharper pain
this one in his groin.
He looked up and he saw
another human being
walking gracefully toward the apple tree.
This human being was essentially like him
though it had features where he lacked them
and others less noticeable.

This human also had a name for herself.
She was "Eve."
Eve laid herself on top of Adam
as the Sun dipped into the night.
Then during that night
Adam and Eve
lying on their backs side by side and arm in arm
far outside the faded circle of the tree
stared in awe at the stars.
They created their own Constellations
making up stories of brave hunters and human heroes
stories they vowed to retell each other
forever and ever.
For they did not yet know that they would die.
Who could know such a thing
in those very first days in the Garden of Eden?
I saw everything that went on there, or here, if you will,
and even I didn't know that someday
I was going to die.

And on the Seventh Day itself
with the rising of the Sun
Adam stood up over Eve.
He took in all that was there
and announced that it was good.
He looked down on Eve and said to her,
"I will be a good lord over all Creation."

Adam and Eve laughed and cried
cried and laughed

both to themselves and the whole world.
And without knowing what was to come
they planned their future
right there and then
or right here and now, if you will
in the Garden of Eden
till the end of time.

They never left the Garden of Eden.
How could they?
It was all there is.

9 781911 221364